Forever Friends

Cedar River Daydreams

Forever Friends

Judy Baer

BETHANY HOUSE PUBLISHERS
MINNEAPOLIS, MINNESOTA 55438

Forever Friends
Copyright © 1999
Judy Baer

Cover illustration by Chris Ellison
Cover design by Sheryl Thornberg

Unless otherwise identified, Scripture quotations are
from *The Holy Bible, New Century Version.* Copyright
© 1987, 1988, 1991 by Word Publishing, Dallas, Texas
75039. Used by permission.

Published by Bethany House Publishers
A Ministry of Bethany Fellowship International
11400 Hampshire Avenue South
Minneapolis, Minnesota 55438
www.bethanyhouse.com

Printed in the United States of America by
Bethany Press International, Minneapolis, Minnesota
55438

**Library of Congress Cataloging-in-Publication
Data**

CIP data applied for

ISBN 1–55661–838–7   CIP

To Sandy Baer—
You said you'd be there for me
and you have been.
I'm more grateful than you'll ever know.

JUDY BAER received a B.A. in English and Education from Concordia College in Moorhead, Minnesota. She has had over fifty novels published and is a member of the National Romance Writers of America, the Society of Children's Book Writers, and the National Federation of Press Women.

Two of her novels, *Adrienne* and *Paige*, have been prizewinning bestsellers for Bethany House. Both books have been awarded first place for juvenile fiction in the National Federation of Press Women's communications contest.

Chapter One

Lexi Leighton dangled her legs over the side of the deck, swinging her feet just over the shrubbery her mother had planted when they'd moved to Cedar River. She braced herself on rigid arms and leaned back to allow the late spring sun to wash over her face.

"It's hard to believe it's almost the end of May," Todd Winston murmured. He was lying on his back, eyes closed, golden hair falling away from his handsome features. "Where did the year go? Where did *last* year go?"

"Homework, the Emerald Tones, homework, school, homework, the *Cedar River Review*, homework . . ."

Todd laughed as he rolled to his stomach. He propped his chin in his hands and watched Lexi. "Never mind, I get it now."

"It *does* seem like only a few months ago that I moved to Cedar River," Lexi admitted pensively. "I thought I'd die of loneliness. Then the Hi-Fives asked me to join their club and I thought my problems were over."

"But they were just beginning." Todd had known the snobbish little group even longer than Lexi.

"I still can't believe they asked me to shoplift as my 'initiation' into their little club. And the way they acted around Ben! They were so ignorant about his disability." Lexi referred to her younger brother, who had Down's syndrome. The Hi-Fives and especially their self-appointed leader, Minda Hannaford, had acted as if they could catch Ben's handicap. It had been a horrible time for Lexi.

"I'm sorry it took you so long to meet the wonderful people—like me," Todd teased.

Lexi gave him a loving look. "And Peggy, Jennifer, Binky, Egg, Anna Marie . . ."

"So it didn't turn out so badly after all," Todd concluded. His hand crept toward Lexi's until they touched.

"Not bad at all."

"What are you two up to?"

Both Todd and Lexi started as Lexi's mother walked onto the porch. She was wiping her hands on a paint-smeared rag. She smelled vaguely of turpentine. An artist and also a victim of multiple sclerosis, Mrs. Leighton took advantage of every day she was feeling well enough to paint.

"Just talking about how quickly time goes by."

Mrs. Leighton laughed. "I thought that was a

conversation only old people like your father and I had!"

"You aren't old!"

"But some days I feel like it. Oh, to be seventeen or eighteen again!" A frown clouded Mrs. Leighton's features. "You kids don't even realize how very young you are, do you?"

Lexi stared at her mother, puzzled. "What do you mean?"

"Oh, never mind." Though Mrs. Leighton brushed off the question, Lexi could tell something was bothering her mother.

"What was that about?" Todd asked after Mrs. Leighton had disappeared into the house.

"I have no idea." Lexi wanted to change the subject. She wanted to think about Todd.

She pulled up her legs and surrounded her knees with her arms. "Remember when I discovered you? That you were my brother's coach? He never called you anything but 'Big Fella' and I had no idea. . . ."

"That he was my 'Little Fellow'?"

"After my horrible experience with the Hi-Fives thinking Ben was some kind of a freak, I was actually scared to introduce him to anyone else in Cedar River." Lexi knocked the heel of her hand against her forehead. "Dumb, dumb, dumb."

"You just got into the wrong crowd at first," Todd said. His eyes narrowed a little. "And went out with Jerry Randall."

"Oh, Jerry wasn't so bad. Just a little conceited is all."

"A little?"

"Well, maybe a lot, but you have to admit he's definitely improved."

"He's a good guy now. But at the time . . ."

"How could I know who was a good friend or a bad one?" Lexi was indignant. "I'd lived in Grover's Point my whole life until I moved here. I'm not a mind reader or anything!"

"You don't have to get so worked up about it," Todd grumbled.

Tension like this between them was practically unheard of. Maybe they'd caught Mrs. Leighton's odd mood.

"I'm just making conversation."

"Well, I don't like the conversation."

Lexi was relieved to see Binky McNaughton coming up the sidewalk. She and Todd were both tense and needed a distraction.

Lexi dismissed the tension and watched Binky walk toward them. It wasn't until Binky was almost to the deck that Lexi realized her friend was crying.

"Binky, what's wrong?" Lexi almost added "now" but didn't. Binky seemed to enjoy living her life going from crisis to crisis. Today, however, she didn't appear to be exaggerating her unhappiness.

"The worst thing just happened!" Binky announced dramatically and threw herself into a lawn chair. "The absolute *worst*. Egg got his ac-

ceptance to that college out East he's been bab-
bling about. He's going to be living in Boston."

"Way to go, Egg!" Todd sat up with a big grin
on his face. "He's been so worried about that ap-
plication. Now he can relax."

"That's great news, Binky," Lexi added. "Ever
since Egg decided he wanted to go into the medical
field, he's been worried about getting into a big
school. So what's the problem?"

"That *is* the problem! Don't you people get it?
Boston is a million miles away. We're never going
to see Egg again."

" 'Never' is pretty strong."

"Maybe not 'never,' but hardly ever. My parents can't afford to pay for airline tickets for him
to go back and forth. He's got grants and scholarships and work-study for school, but he can't use
it for travel." Binky's impish little face was for-
lorn. "Why didn't he just decide to go to the junior
college here, like he'd first planned?"

"You and Egg fight all the time anyway, Binky.
Maybe you'll be glad when he's gone," Todd
pointed out matter-of-factly. The McNaughtons
seemed to *look* for things to disagree over.

"But that's what's fun, don't you see? Egg and
I have this . . . understanding. We agree to disagree." Binky blushed to the roots of her hair as she
admitted, "It's kind of the way we show that we
love each other." Tears filled her eyes. "Dumb,
huh?"

"I think your friends have always known that,"

Lexi said gently. "And we'll all miss Egg."

Binky's jaw jutted out and she got an expression of determination on her features like only Binky could have. "I'm not going to miss him. I'm not going to let myself. If he's not smart enough to see that he should stay closer to his family and friends, then I'd be crazy to miss him. I'm just going to be mad at him."

One big tear rolled down her cheek and then another until Binky looked like a human waterfall.

"It's all ending, don't you see?" Binky's resolution to be angry with Egg was already history. "Things will never be the same! First Egg leaves. Next year it's the rest of us. We'll all go to faraway places like Boston or Los Angeles or Norway. . . ."

Lexi and Todd both did a double take at Binky's mention of Norway, although it sounded like a pretty cool place to go.

"We won't see each other anymore. It will be too expensive to talk on the phone, we're all lousy at writing, and I know everyone won't bother to email. Oh, at first we might try to stay in touch, but it will be less and less often. Then it will be only at Christmastime and our high school reunions. Pretty soon we'll be our parents' ages and not even recognize one another. We'll be fat and bald and have wrinkles! Why can't things just stay the way they are now?"

"Aren't you exaggerating just a little? We'll always be friends even if we aren't together," Todd said. "Friends can stay friends even if they're miles apart."

Binky looked doubtful, as if she wanted to believe what Todd said was true but knew in her heart that she was right.

Lexi didn't say a word. She couldn't think of a thing that might console Binky. Maybe Binky was right. Maybe things would never be the same between any of them after Egg's graduation.

"Hey, Lexi, what's happenin'?"

Lexi looked up from her textbook at her brother, Ben, in shock. " 'What's happenin'?' Where did you hear that?"

"On a rerun on television." Ben dropped into a chair beside his sister. His dark, silky hair was cropped short now. He'd gone to Todd's barber, and the new cut made him look much older. His round face was still sweet and his dark, almond-shaped eyes twinkled, but he was growing up—something Lexi was having a hard time getting used to. He was her *baby* brother. Had he forgotten?

Ben had blossomed at the Academy for the Handicapped. Some Down's syndrome children could learn to read and write. Ben was one of the fortunate ones. He was high functioning, and his confidence and charm were growing every day.

"Lexi?"

"Yes, Ben?" She closed the book to give him her full attention.

"I've got a girlfriend." His cheeks turned pink, and he looked away from her as if afraid she'd read something in his eyes.

"You've always had girlfriends. Dozens of them. You're a hunk, little bro."

"But *I* like this one."

"Benjamin! Can I believe what I'm hearing?"

Ben blushed and backed toward the door. The silly grin on his face told Lexi she could indeed believe his words.

After he left, his words truly sunk in and the revelation hit Lexi like a blow. Her mind flashed through a series of memories as if they were from a photo album in her mind. Ben, being taunted by the Hi-Fives when the Leightons had first moved to Cedar River. Ben, getting lost. Ben, charming her friends Peggy, Binky, and Jennifer. Ben, with his new puppy, Wiggles, playing on the grass. Ben, always there for her, sympathetic and loving, even if he didn't know exactly what was wrong or what to do about her problems. And now this Ben— taller and more mature with his new haircut and new confidence . . . and a girlfriend?

Binky was right. Things would never stay the same. In fact, they'd changed already, right under Lexi's nose, and she hadn't noticed it until now. Everyone was growing up and growing apart. Suddenly she felt as teary eyed and melancholy as Binky had been.

Lexi pushed away from the table as her mother

entered the room. There was someone she needed to see.

"Where are you going, Lexi?"

"To see Grandma. Is there anything you'd like me to take to her, Mom?"

Mrs. Leighton shook her head. "I don't think so. She is by nature so generous that anything we take to her there she tries to give away. Some of the residents of the nursing home aren't supposed to have candy. She got in trouble last week for giving a diabetic that box of chocolate-covered cherries I brought her."

"So Grandma's a troublemaker?" Lexi giggled. "What a thought!"

"Well, it's hardly her fault. Alzheimer's does horrible things to one's mind." Mrs. Leighton picked a photograph off the counter. "Give her this. It's a picture of you and Ben. You can help her put it into her photo album. I know she won't give that away. Even though her mind is foggy, she knows the faces in those pictures are precious to her."

As Lexi drove toward the nursing home, she felt strangely comforted by her mother's comment. *"The faces in those pictures are precious to her."*

Even though Grandma's memory had been stolen from her by the disease, she still knew that there were those who loved her. It was going to be like that for Lexi and her friends, too. They didn't have to be together to know they were cared about.

And a telephone was always just an arm's length away.

She was going to have to straighten out Binky before she depressed everyone unnecessarily, Lexi decided. Binky was quite the prophetess of doom. True, their lives were changing, but maybe they would only get better.

———

"Mortarboard, gown, new suit, new shoes, new haircut . . ." Egg ticked off the items he needed for his big day.

"New underwear," Jennifer Golden added. "And, please, new socks."

"What's wrong with my socks?" Egg stuck out a leg so that everyone could see his thin ankle and the garish red-and-yellow pattern of his stocking. "I've got several pairs just like this. They were on sale at Discount Mart."

"I wonder why," Jennifer mumbled. "Maybe because they were scaring customers at the retail stores."

"College students need to be economical. I'll have a lot more expenses now that I'm going to be on my own."

"Oh, give it a rest, Egg," Binky growled. "You've got enough financial aid and loans to pay for everything except what you had to pay for at home. You're going to have a cool dorm room, three meals a day, and a whole new life! The rest of us are still stuck in high school."

"Do I detect a note of jealousy?" Egg asked arrogantly. "From the sister who has said for the last four years that she can hardly wait until I leave home so she can have my room?"

"I don't want your room anymore. I think it's got lice or something."

"Okay, you two," Todd said with a sigh. "Let's get back to the reason we're all here." He gestured at the room filled with their friends—Lexi, Peggy Madison, Anna Marie Arnold, Jerry Randall, Matt Windsor, Tim Anders, and Angela Hardy. "We're supposed to be planning a combination graduation and moving party for you, not fighting over who gets your room."

"I don't feel like it," Angela announced. "It's too sad. I agree with Binky."

"That's because you're Egg's girlfriend," Jerry pointed out matter-of-factly. "Not that I've ever understood what you see in him, but I suppose in some weird way you'll miss him."

" 'Weird way'?" Egg echoed. "What do you mean?"

"You've got to admit you're one of a kind, Eggo. There's no one else quite like you."

"He means you're *special*, Egg," Angela said as she put her hand on his arm. "Very special."

Jerry rolled his eyes but didn't argue.

Egg looked pleased. "I am?"

"Everyone here is special in some way," said Lexi. I remember moving here from Grover's Point and being afraid that I'd never make a friend, that there'd be no one I liked who would like me." She made an all-encompassing gesture with her arms. "And look at all the friends I have now!"

"You were the one who helped me when I first discovered I had dyslexia," Jennifer said. She shook her head as if she couldn't believe how she'd behaved in the past. "I sure did a lot of dumb things back then. Remember when I chopped off all my hair?"

Matt winced. "It was just a phase."

Lexi smiled to herself. Matt had come a long way from the angry, unsmiling guy with flat black eyes and an aura of badness about him. He'd made peace with his stepmother and accepted the fact that his mother and sister had moved away. He'd also found an even more important relationship— one with Jesus Christ—that had mellowed him. The sullen bad boy smiled often now. He'd quit smoking, fighting, and running with the wrong crowd.

"I remember Lexi's 'phase,'" Binky announced smugly. "She isn't always perfect, you know."

"I never said I was!"

"But you do everything right most of the time," Binky responded. "Except when your parents had that foster girl. What was her name?"

"Amanda. Amanda Remer." Lexi's mind flew back to the days when Amanda lived at her house. Amanda had nearly driven her wild with her heart-shaped face and large brown eyes. She had acted so sweet and innocent to everyone except

Lexi. Amanda was a chameleon who changed colors depending on whom she was around. If Todd or anyone else popular, influential, male, or otherwise interesting was nearby, she could charm them fully. It was only when she and Lexi were alone that she showed her dark, jealous side. A former runaway from a home of alcoholic parents, Amanda was jealous of Lexi's happy homelife and had done everything in her power to make Lexi miserable. Most of the time she had succeeded.

"Do you ever hear from her?" Peggy asked.

"Once in a while," Lexi answered. "It's funny, but I consider her a real friend now. There was a time when I couldn't even stand to have her in my house."

"Hey! I thought we were talking about *me*, how *I'm* special," Egg protested. He'd gone into the kitchen for food and come back carrying a large bowl of chips and a container of dip.

"We're just reminiscing about old times," Lexi said.

"I remember something special about Egg," Jennifer said slyly. "Remember when he decided to lift weights and was stupid enough to consider taking steroids to help him bulk up?"

"I don't want to talk about that," Egg growled. "Besides, I've decided that my body is perfect the way it is."

"You're right," Todd agreed without missing a beat. "You are a long, lean eating machine."

Egg grinned and stuffed a chip in his mouth. "Right. Cool, huh?"

"You did start that big environmental campaign to clean up Cedar River," Jennifer admitted.

"And the 'brick in every toilet' fiasco," Binky added. Everyone was laughing now.

"We've had some good times together," Todd concluded. "It won't be the same around here without you, Egg."

"Better, maybe," Jerry teased, but the joke fell flat as Binky burst into tears and ran out of the room.

————

Lexi found Binky upstairs, sprawled across a bed, bawling her eyes out.

"Binky?"

"Go away."

"I don't think so." Lexi sat down on the bed opposite her friend and clutched a pillow to her midsection. "I'll just stay here till you're done crying. Then we'll go back downstairs."

"You'll be here all night" came the muffled warning.

"I doubt it. You'll run out of tears. Besides, Egg's going to school, not dying or anything."

Binky rolled to her back, and her tear-swollen eyes stared accusingly at Lexi. "Can't you *feel* it?"

"Feel what?"

"Things changing. Lexi, we've had so much fun together. I don't want it to stop. Sure, it's just Egg going away now, but *next* year . . ."

So that was it. Binky was already worrying about her own future.

"Sure we've had fun. And we'll have more. But high school hasn't been perfect. Chad committed suicide. Todd had that terrible football accident. Minda Hannaford and the Hi-Fives nearly drove us crazy. You can't tell me that's all been fun!"

"No," Binky said reluctantly. "Maybe my memory filters out the bad stuff, but I don't care. I like things the way they are."

"Nothing stays the same. Nothing but God, that is. What does it say in Hebrews? Something about God's 'unchangeable purpose.' Everything He promises is unchanging and true, but you can't count on anything else to stay the same.

"Besides," Lexi continued thoughtfully, "I'm kind of glad our lives change. We'd be awfully bored if we were stuck in high school forever. Egg's looking forward to college, and you should be happy for him."

"Get over the pity party, you mean?" Binky sat up, grabbed a tissue from the bedside table, and blew her nose. Her cheeks were pink and swollen, her nose bright red.

"Something like that. You can't change it. All you can change is your attitude, you know."

Binky thought about that statement for a moment. "You mean find something good about Egg leaving, all my friends going separate directions, and getting old?"

"At least about Egg's going to college. That would be a start."

Binky screwed her face into a thoughtful expression. "Well, he *does* have a bigger room than mine. With more windows. And a walk-in closet. He won't be needing that much space now. I guess there's no reason *I* couldn't move out of my dinky room into that one. . . . And he's got a queen-sized bed. I wonder if Mom and Dad are going to let him take the computer to school or if he has to leave it home for me. . . ."

Lexi laughed out loud. "That's what I like about you, Binky. Your mind can switch gears in a second if it has to. Come on, let's go downstairs and see what's happening with everyone else. You've probably got them all so depressed that you'll have to cheer *them* up!"

Arm in arm, the girls made their way back to the living room.

Chapter Two

"People, will you please be quiet!" Mrs. Waverly rapped her conductor's stick on the edge of a music stand. "I realize you think you're already out of school for the summer, but you aren't and won't be for some time yet. We have a lot of work to do before graduation."

Amidst groans and muttered complaints, the chorus students found their chairs. The music room was warm today, and the air conditioner was not working properly. It was hard to pay attention.

"First, I'd like to hear the seniors sing the vocal selection they've chosen to present at graduation." Mrs. Waverly's hair was, as usual, stacked on top of her head and tilting slightly. It sprouted more than the usual number of pencils, and tendrils of curls softened her face. It was obvious as she smiled that she was very fond of this group of seniors.

They separated themselves from the rest of the group and gave a halfhearted rendition of the selection. Mrs. Waverly frowned but said only, "I'm sure you'll be more enthusiastic on graduation day."

Lexi doubted it. Everyone was so emotional, it would be a miracle if they got any words out of their mouths at all. Even the Emerald Tones were having trouble with the selections they would sing. Once the impressive strains of "Pomp and Circumstance" started to play and the graduates began walking down the aisle, everyone would be a total mess.

She glanced at Binky, who was starting to be a total mess far too early. Tears dripped down Binky's cheeks, and her lips trembled. That attitude adjustment Lexi had advocated hadn't lasted long. She'd have to try again later.

Mrs. Waverly gave another rap on the music stand. "Now, if you'd all sit down, I have a surprise for you."

Whistles and surprised whoops filled the air. Mrs. Waverly was usually pretty no-nonsense in class. "Now, close your eyes and don't peek."

Muttered questions came from all parts of the room. Lexi and Todd glanced questioningly at each other. What was Mrs. Waverly up to? She was everyone's favorite teacher, but this was unusual, even for her.

A commotion in the hall was followed by the sound of rolling wheels and secretive whispers. Finally Mrs. Waverly clapped her hands and said, "Okay, you may open your eyes now."

At first, Lexi thought the podium had caught fire.

A huge graduation cake, blazing with sparklers, sat in front of them on one of the stainless steel carts from the cafeteria. A second cart held two large insulated beverage dispensers and cafeteria plates, forks, and glasses.

"Is that for us?" Egg asked, his eyes wide.

"I thought we'd better have our celebration early," Mrs. Waverly responded with a smile. "If I couldn't offer you the biggest party in appreciation for all your class has contributed to the music department these past four years, at least I could have the first. Now, who's going to cut the cake?"

It was a chocolate-and-yellow marble cake with half-inch-thick fudge frosting. It disappeared, along with the two dispensers of milk, in a matter of minutes. Then the students, who'd decided to sit on the floor and the risers instead of in their chairs, began to reminisce.

"Remember that time Egg fell off the top riser during our big finale? He got so into the music, he didn't realize he'd stepped backward until he fell flat on his back."

"And got the wind knocked out of him," Todd added. "We guys tried to close up the space Eggo had vacated, but we couldn't do anything about the noise he was making trying to catch his breath."

"He sounded like a dying cow," Minda Hannaford said, turning up her nose. "It was humiliating."

"I could have been killed!" Egg protested. "Wasn't anyone worried about me?"

"Nah," Jerry said. "We figured you'd hit your head first, and we knew there was nothing up there that could be damaged."

"And remember how, once he recovered, he crawled back onto the riser and just sort of appeared again? The whole audience burst out laughing!" Tim snickered.

"You're one to talk," Egg retorted, turning his attention to Tim. "I remember the time in junior high chorus when you had that solo and—"

"My voice was changing, okay?" Tim blushed. "I couldn't help it."

"The sound you made could have broken glass!" Gina Williams giggled. *"Screeeeeech!"*

"I remember the time Anna Marie fainted," Tressa offered. "You were dieting too hard and . . . boom!"

"I always ate something before a concert after that," Anna Marie admitted. "I'm glad those days are over, though." She was referring to her bouts with anorexia and bulimia. Now she was a normal, healthy weight and happier than she'd ever been.

"Minda, remember the time at the vocal contest when the judge told you that you'd be better off 'pursuing something you were better at, like mathematics'?" Jennifer liked to get a dig in at

Minda as often as possible.

Minda dismissed the question with a ladylike snort. "And Mrs. Waverly complained about that judge, and he was never asked back to the contest. Fortunately, I knew my own talent. If he'd said something like that to you, he might have crushed you for life."

"Yeah, right."

The banter continued until the class bell rang and the students drifted reluctantly out of the room to their next class. Lexi and Binky, who had study hall next period, offered to stay behind and help clean up the mess.

Binky carried a garbage bag and collected napkins while Lexi and Mrs. Waverly picked up utensils and swept up crumbs.

"This was really nice of you," Lexi offered. "What a great idea."

"I've thought about doing it for years," Mrs. Waverly said, "but this year I just felt I had to start. This senior class has been very special to me—just as next year's graduating class has been. I'm going to miss you all."

A tearful hiccup punctuated the silence after Mrs. Waverly's comment. Binky was stuffing paper into the bag and crying.

"Oh, Bink . . ." Lexi was beginning to feel helpless to do anything for her friend. Binky was weeping at practically everything lately.

Mrs. Waverly gave Lexi an inquiring look, and Lexi shrugged helplessly. "It's been this way for days. It's hit her hard that Egg is graduating and moving away. She's realizing that we will be next—going to college, moving in different directions, perhaps losing track of one another. Binky isn't good with change."

"Come here, dear," Mrs. Waverly ordered. She patted the seat of a chair and sat down in one across from it. Binky reluctantly put down the garbage bag and trailed over. Feeling awkward, Lexi picked it up and kept herself busy.

"Nothing stays the same, my dear," Mrs. Waverly began. "And we wouldn't want it that way."

"I would," Binky said stubbornly.

"If things never changed, Lexi never would have left Grover's Point and moved to Cedar River," the teacher said logically.

"That's different," sniffled Binky.

"Not really." Lexi had to interrupt. "I didn't want to leave. I cried and cried. I left all my good friends behind."

"But we were here!" Binky protested.

"I didn't know that. All I knew was that I was losing something. I had no idea how much I would be gaining. Now I'm *happy* we moved, but at the time, you couldn't have convinced me of that for anything."

"So you think I'm going to *like* having Egg gone?"

"You do fight a lot, you know."

"But what about next year? When I lose everyone?"

"The post office won't close. We have telephones and email. You and Harry have been able to keep up a long-distance friendship." Lexi referred to Binky's sometimes boyfriend who was at college. "And all our parents live here. We'll be home for holidays and summers, most likely."

"Maybe, but it won't be the same." Binky was being persistent.

"Perhaps it will be *better*," Mrs. Waverly suggested. "You'll all have so much to share about what you've been doing and studying."

"Maybe." Binky was doubtful but seemed to be coming around to Mrs. Waverly's optimism.

"You'll have new friends coming home with you to introduce to—"

"I want my *old* friends!" Binky wailed. "That's it, don't you see? What if I can't make new friends? Everybody here is used to me."

"You don't take so much getting used to, Binky," Lexi said, coloring the truth just a little.

"Hah!"

"And you are one of the sweetest people I've ever known." That was the honest truth. Lexi had grown to love Binky in the time she'd known her.

"You're just lacking confidence right now," Mrs. Waverly concluded. "Egg has been your confidant and protector for a long time, and now he's leaving. But you are a very capable girl, Binky. More capable than you realize."

"I am?" Binky sounded amazed.

"Give yourself some credit," Mrs. Waverly encouraged. "You'll be surprised what wonderful things are in the future."

Binky pondered that statement and began to nod slowly. "Yeah. Great things." Then a tear slipped down her cheek. "But I still want the great things to happen with my brother and my friends."

———

"Let's stop at Peggy's," Lexi suggested as she and Jennifer drove home from the mall. "It seems like we haven't talked in ages."

"Too much going on." Jennifer pulled her car into Peggy's driveway. "I feel like I've been drowning in final projects and tests. Of course, I finish things twice as slowly as anyone else."

"Hi!" Peggy appeared from around the corner of the house, carrying a pail of water, which she dumped into a large planter by the front steps. "What are you two up to?"

"We came to see you. What's up?"

"Not much. Mom handed me a list of chores as soon as I walked in the door. She said I hadn't been home enough in the past two weeks to help out. This is the last of the list." Peggy dropped the bucket with a clatter. "Want to come inside?"

"She won't put us to work, will she?" Jennifer asked wryly. "My mother caught me yesterday."

Mrs. Madison smiled when the girls entered the kitchen. "You're just in time."

"Uh-oh," Jennifer muttered.

"For fresh caramel rolls. Interested?"

"Oh, they smell great!" Jennifer bellied up to the counter.

After piling a tray high with rolls and glasses of milk, Peggy led the girls into the family room. She moved a stack of magazines to one side to make room for the food.

"Have either of you seen Binky today?" Peggy asked.

"Just in class. She bolted out as soon as the bell rang. Why?" Lexi said.

"She's acting weird, that's all. I thought she'd be getting used to Egg's graduating by now, but she seems to be getting worse." Peggy's forehead furrowed into a troubled line. "I wish she were feeling happier about the whole thing."

"She's taking Egg's leaving harder than I expected," Jennifer agreed. "After all, they argue constantly. Who'd miss that?"

"That's their fun," Lexi pointed out. "That's how they communicate."

"I just hope she cheers up soon." Peggy looked almost as miserable as Binky had been appearing.

"Why are *you* so worried?" Jennifer asked with her usual bluntness. "Binky has these crazy phases all the time. What makes this any different?"

"Because *I* have some news to tell her, too.

And until she has a better attitude, I don't dare say anything."

Lexi and Jennifer both straightened at Peggy's mysterious statement, the rolls and milk forgotten.

"What kind of news?" Jennifer's eyes narrowed suspiciously. The last big news Peggy had told them was that she was pregnant with her boyfriend Chad's baby.

Peggy instinctively seemed to know what her friends were thinking. "Not *that* kind of news! Don't you think I learned my lesson?" Her eyes filled with unshed tears.

"What kind of news, then?" Jennifer persisted. Lexi remained quiet.

"My family is moving at the end of the school year."

"No way!"

"Why?"

"You *can't*!"

"I know. I said the same thing, but Dad got this great job offer that he says he can't pass up. I begged and begged to stay here just one more year so I could graduate with my class, but Mom doesn't want us to be separated, and it *is* a great job. It's something he's wanted to do all his life. Dad has been walking around with a smile on his face for two weeks."

"No wonder you're worried about Binky!" Jennifer blurted. "This is going to blow her away. First Egg, now you."

"Tell me about it." Peggy flung herself back against the couch. "The *last* thing I want to do is make things worse for Binky." Her face softened. "Or for any of you. You've been the best friends a girl could ever have. You all stood by me after Chad died. And when it came out that I'd been pregnant and had given the baby away, none of you said or did anything to make me feel worse than I already did."

They were all silent a moment, and then Peggy continued. "When I broke up with Chad and he committed suicide, I was devastated. We *all* were. But even at the worst time in my life, I knew God was with me. I *felt* Him. He carried me when I couldn't walk on my own."

"He made a miracle," Lexi whispered.

Peggy stared out the window, her mind obviously a million miles away. "It's funny, but the idea of moving has made me think about the baby. In the back of my mind, I suppose I thought maybe . . . someday . . . she might try to find me. That happens sometimes, you know. But if we move, it will make it so much harder. . . ." Tears spilled down Peggy's cheeks.

"But how would she find you anyway?" Jennifer asked.

"I left it in her file that she could look me up," Peggy said. "I wrote her a letter and explained why I couldn't keep her. I wanted her to know I loved her."

"That will be a wait," Jennifer muttered.

"Probably at least until she's in college."

"I know. That's why I'm thinking of going on the Web."

The girls stared at Peggy. "The Internet?" Lexi finally asked. "What good will that do?"

"I read about a couple who found a baby to adopt on the Web," Peggy explained. "Did you know that there are tons of listings for different topics about adoptions? It's really cool. You can find out about special-needs children, older kids in need of homes, and places to go to ask questions about getting through the adoption process more quickly. There are even pictures of children waiting to be adopted!

"And," she added softly, "a message board for birth parents who want to find the children they've put up for adoption."

"It would be pretty freaky to find each other that way," Jennifer observed.

"I know. Besides, I'm not even sure I *want* to find her new parents. I just think about the 'what ifs.' "

"You'll find her if you are supposed to," Lexi said. "God has a way of working things out. I really believe that."

"I know. I believe it, too." Peggy sighed. "It's just so hard."

"Do you want the baby back?" Jennifer asked bluntly.

"Oh no. I did the right thing for both of us at the time. I was so young. I still am! I just want to know my baby is well and happy."

On the way home, Jennifer asked, "Do you think she means it? Or do you think she wants more—like to *see* the baby?"

"I have no idea," Lexi said. "I've never been in Peggy's position. I don't envy her."

"And I don't envy her when she has to tell Binky she's moving." Jennifer gave a low whistle. "Then the emotional fireworks will start!"

———

"Why the long face?" Mrs. Leighton inquired. Lexi sat on a chair at the kitchen table silently toying with the fringe on a place mat, her expression indicating her thoughts were somber ones.

"Everything is getting messed up, that's all."

" 'Everything'? Just exactly what does that include?" Mrs. Leighton pulled out a chair and sat down across from her daughter.

"You know . . . my friends. I didn't realize how much Egg's graduation would affect us all. The rest of the gang has only one year left, and then we'll be going away to school, as well. And Peggy just told me and Jennifer that she's moving this spring!"

"So her father took that job," Mrs. Leighton mused.

"You *knew* about it?"

"Her mother said they were considering it but

didn't want it to get out until they had made a final decision."

"It's horrible, Mom. Egg. Peggy. My senior year is going to be awful!"

"Hardly. You have many wonderful friends. And you know as well as anyone, Lexi, that things just don't stay the same. In fact, you wouldn't want them to."

"Binky does. And I'm beginning to think I do, too."

Mrs. Leighton's face took on a somber, unreadable expression—one Lexi had not seen before.

"Since we're having this conversation, there is something else I'd like to discuss with you, Lexi."

Lexi felt a shock of alarm go through her. Her mom rarely looked or sounded so serious. "Are you feeling okay? Is your multiple sclerosis flaring up?"

"No. I feel fine. This has nothing to do with my health. It's something your father and I have been discussing recently."

Now Lexi was truly puzzled.

Mrs. Leighton took a deep breath. "Lexi, you and Todd have been together a long time."

"So?"

"I know that you two are the best of friends. Your brother adores him, and your father and I think of him practically as a son."

"That's great, but . . ." What was her mother trying to get at?

"Dad and I feel that your relationship with Todd has been changing gradually."

"How?"

"We think it's turned into something . . . much more romantic than it used to be."

Lexi blushed but didn't argue. They *were* boyfriend and girlfriend, after all. That was no surprise to anyone.

"Dad and I feel that it would be better if you and Todd began seeing others. To us it seems you spend too much time with Todd."

"But he's my best friend!" Lexi burst out.

"And your boyfriend. You are both very young. Neither of you needs to be so tied down. It would be healthier if you dated others, as well."

"We aren't 'tied down'! We *want* to be together."

"That's my point, Lexi. We see you getting a little too serious about each other."

"What's wrong with that?" Lexi asked belligerently.

"Nothing—if you were older. But you are high school students. You have another year of school left. If you and Todd date each other exclusively, you won't make other friends."

"We have other friends. Lots of them." Lexi glared at her mother. "What you're saying is that you don't want something to happen to Todd and me like what happened to Peggy and Chad."

Mrs. Leighton sighed. "Lexi, I trust both of you. I believe that you both saw how devastating an out-of-wedlock pregnancy can be. I just don't want you to be hurt or to miss the freedom of your high school years because you are so attached to one young man."

Lexi felt sick inside. She couldn't believe her mother was saying this to her. "But what would I do without him?"

"Your father and I think it's time you found out." Mrs. Leighton's voice was firm. "We want you to start dating other people. No more exclusivity— at least not for a while."

"So you want me to break up with Todd? Just like that?"

"I'll talk to him if you like."

"No!" Lexi was on the verge of tears. "You can't do this to us! We belong together!"

Mrs. Leighton remained calm. "Perhaps you do. And if that is true, then I fully believe that you *will* be together. If it's God's will, then it'll happen. That knowledge will come through prayer and listening for His advice. But for now your father and I think it best that you and Todd see less of each other and spend less time alone together."

"No!" Lexi cried, tears streaming down her cheeks. "You can't . . . we can't—"

"Your father will talk to you tonight, Lexi,"

Mrs. Leighton said. "I know this is difficult but . . ."

Difficult? It was *impossible*! Lexi pushed back her chair and ran to her room sobbing.

Chapter Three

Lexi had been in her room crying ever since her talk with her mother. Mrs. Leighton had left Lexi alone with her thoughts as she attempted to absorb this crushing blow her parents had dealt her.

She'd felt every emotion possible, she decided—anger, rage, fury, disbelief, pain, and grief—as the minutes ticked on like hours. Each time Lexi heard a car go by, she jumped to look out the window to see if it was her father coming home. It was never him.

How could they do this to her? Why were they so suspicious and untrusting? Didn't they understand anything? Lexi had never been so angry with her parents in her entire life—not even when they'd announced that they were leaving Grover's Point to move to Cedar River. And she'd thought her life was falling apart *then*! Little had she known!

But maybe this was all her mother's idea, Lexi rationalized. Maybe Dad had just gone along with the silly idea to keep her happy. Surely Dad would make sense even if her mother . . .

Lexi heard the crunch of tires on the driveway and the sound of a car door slamming shut. Her father was home.

She could smell squash with cinnamon and brown sugar baking and the aroma of steaming ham and scalloped potatoes—one of her favorite meals.

Bribery. But a good meal was not going to put her off. Her mother couldn't cook away this problem.

Lexi's father was waiting for her at the bottom of the stairs. "Hello, honey."

"Daddy—" Her voice broke and she threw herself into his arms.

"I take it your mother talked to you about our decision?"

"*Her* decision."

"No, sweetheart, *our* decision. One we made together."

"But, Dad . . ."

Lexi was devastated. Her father couldn't betray her, too!

"Let's sit down in the living room," Dr. Leighton suggested gently. "We need to talk."

Lexi held back. "I don't want to talk. You're both wrong. Todd and I aren't getting too serious about each other. We just like to be together, that's all."

"I know, Lexi, but it's not good parenting if we don't point out to you the dangers of an exclusive

relationship at your age with someone of the opposite sex."

"Okay. So you've pointed it out. We won't do
anything wrong—not that we were planning to
anyway. You and Mom can just relax, and we can
forget about this whole conversation. Right?" A
hopeful quaver punctuated her question.

"Lexi, we trust both you and Todd, but we don't
think it's healthy for you to be so exclusive. You'll
both be seniors next year. That's a time to be free
to make new friends."

"I don't *want* new friends! I like the ones I
have. Egg is graduating, Peggy is moving—I can't
lose Todd, too!"

"I understand how you feel, but—"

"No, you don't! You couldn't. You just couldn't!"
Wracking with sobs, Lexi ran upstairs to her bedroom and flung herself across the bed.

———

"Lexi? You in there?" Ben's hesitant voice fil-
tered through the door. "Mom saved supper for
you."

Lexi sat up and rubbed at eyes that stung from
crying. She glanced at the clock on her bedside
stand. It was after nine. She had cried herself to
sleep.

"I'm not hungry." Her throat was sore, and she
wished for a glass of water, but she didn't want to
face Ben. He didn't need to see her like this, all
blotchy and red from crying.

"Are you sick?"

"Sort of." *Sick at heart,* she added to herself. "Don't worry about me, Ben. Go to bed."

"Night, Lexi."

"Good night, Ben." She heard his slippered footsteps padding down the hall and his door close after him. Shortly, one of her parents came up to tuck him into bed. There was no knock at her door, however.

Lexi knew what that meant. Her parents were deadly serious about her and Todd. They were giving her time to "come to her senses," as her father might say. That was not a good sign. Seldom did her parents have to take a firm stance, but when they did, she'd never been able to divert them.

A rush of anger flooded through her. *How dare they do this to me!* She was almost a senior in high school! She'd be in college in another eighteen months! Then they wouldn't be able to control her. Didn't they trust her at all?

Lexi stomped around her room, fuming and thinking all sorts of unpleasant things. As she was plotting and planning her way around this new problem, her eyes fell on the Bible on the bedside stand.

Shame washed over her. Where had her faith gone when her parents confronted her? Out the window. Lexi had forgotten all about God. What would He do about this? What would He say? Hands shaking, she reached for her Bible.

Her mind was a whirl as she stared at the

Book. She had no idea where to search first for an answer to her questions. Finally Lexi turned to the concordance at the back of the Bible and looked there for verses that referred to parents. There were several. First jotting down the Scripture passages, Lexi began to search the Word to see what God would have to say about parents—hers in particular.

Honor your father and your mother. The words of Exodus seemed to leap off the page at her as though the Lord were speaking directly to her. *Honor.* She knew what that word meant—to respect. To respect her parents' wishes? Lexi wasn't ready to accept that. Her parents were wrong. She was sure of it. Wasn't she?

Her fingers flew to find another verse, one more to her liking. The next on her list was Proverbs 3:12. *"The Lord corrects those he loves, just as parents correct the child they delight in."*

Lexi frowned. This wasn't working out the way she'd planned at all. Proverbs 29:15 didn't make her any happier, either. *"Correction and punishment make children wise, but those left alone will disgrace their mother."*

These verses made it sound as though her parents were doing the right thing to guide, direct, and correct her. Her parents were following God's Word to the letter.

And what about her? Was she honoring their efforts like she was supposed to?

Nothing was working out! Absolutely nothing.

If she was to do the right thing—the thing God wanted her to do—she would listen to her parents. She knew them well enough to realize that they hadn't taken this stance on her relationship with Todd quickly. They always prayed about big decisions. Sometimes they even went to Pastor Lake to ask his opinion on things.

And she knew what Pastor Lake would say about this. "Respect your parents, Lexi. Honor them as the Lord wants you to."

But she was already losing Egg and Peggy. She didn't want to let go of Todd, too!

———

The gang met at their usual table in the cafeteria. Egg came breezing in last, just having spent the last hour in a class meeting discussing graduation plans.

He had a big grin on his face when he announced, "Guess what? I was chosen to give one of the symposium speeches at graduation!"

"All right, Eggo!" Todd said.

"That's great, Egg," Matt Windsor echoed.

"Now your head will be too big to get through a door," Jennifer said.

The symposium speeches were given by three students representative of the class. Usually they included the most involved students in different areas—sports, music, academics—or sometimes a student was chosen for his or her popularity or speaking skills.

"Why'd they pick *you*?" Binky growled in a vain attempt to burst Egg's joy.

"Because they said I'd do a great job and that there was no one else like me. I ran the student store, organized an environmental campaign, sang with the Emerald Tones, worked on the school newspaper, and a bunch of other stuff."

"I'd have to agree," Lexi said. "There is no one else like Egg. If they want someone unique, there's no other choice."

"Definitely one of a kind. Congratulations, Egg," Peggy said.

Binky looked sour as a pickle, with her arms crossed and her faced screwed into a scowl at this new reminder that things were changing.

Then Egg hit them with another blow.

"And I've got even *better* news! I've decided to go to summer school!"

"What?" Binky's voice was so high pitched it could have broken glass. "Since when?"

"Since my meeting with the guidance counselor today. I applied for a grant, and it came through this morning. I can have my summer's tuition paid for—isn't that terrific? I called Mom and Dad. They think it's great because it will save us big bucks, and with Binky graduating and going to college next year . . ."

"You don't have to leave now because of *me*," Binky protested, horrified.

"I know, but it will make things easier for Mom and Dad. Besides, I'm looking forward to it. I'm ready to move on. I'll be staying in the dorm and will have the opportunity to learn the campus so I won't look like a dumb freshman next fall. Cool, huh?"

Binky looked as if Egg had hit her over the head with a plank. Lexi jumped into the silence. "When will you move?"

"Right after graduation." Mom and Dad both offered to take time off from work. Binky can help me pack. No sweat. I can be ready."

"Don't count on it."

Egg stared at his sister. "What do you mean? You told me months ago you'd help me pack for college."

"That was before you were actually *doing* it. And now you're planning to go even earlier. There's no way I'm helping you leave me behind."

"Binky, get over it. I'm a senior. . . ."

Binky rolled her eyes. "Don't I know! I've been hearing it often enough! Senior pictures. Senior graduation announcements. Senior parties. Senior honors night. Blech!"

"You should be happy for him," Peggy pointed out a little timidly.

"Happy? Of course I'm happy. Can't you tell?" Binky was in a fury.

"Not really," Jennifer muttered.

"But I'd be a lot *happier* if he just went to the local junior college like he'd planned all along. You promised, Egg!"

Egg's expression was half worry, half irritation. "I can go to a bigger, better school for less money because of the scholarships and grants available to me. The junior college just couldn't offer as much. Besides, you're graduating next year. And all your friends will be here to graduate with you."

"He's going to school, not dying," Jennifer pointed out with her usual bluntness. "He'll probably be back so often we'll get sick of him."

"That's not it," Binky choked. The tears that had formed in her eyes began to spill down her cheeks. "It's not just Egg. It's everyone. I like things the way they are. I don't want anything to change."

No one spoke. There was no way to make Binky's wish come true.

————

"Want a ride home?" Todd caught up with Lexi in the hallway.

Lexi's breath caught in her throat. "Sure. But only if you have some extra time. There's something we need to talk about."

"Fine. I don't have any other plans." Todd took her hand as they walked together to his car.

Lexi loved that old car almost as much as Todd did. He'd refurbished it and kept it in good running order. They'd traveled so many miles and had so much fun with that old thing.

Tears welled unexpectedly in Lexi's eyes as the car brought back a flood of memories of the past two years. If it was going to be this hard to part with a car, how could she ever tell Todd that her parents wanted them to break up?

"Lexi?" Todd looked worried. "Something wrong?"

"Let's sit down." Without waiting for him, she slid into the passenger seat of the car and nestled down into the velvety cushion. The car smelled of Todd's cologne. She inhaled deeply, and more tears surfaced.

"What's happened?" He took her hand and held it to his cheek. The gentle gesture caused Lexi to break into sobs.

When she could finally speak, Lexi blurted, "It's my parents, Todd. They want us to break up!"

He stared at her, puzzled, as if he hadn't quite heard what she'd said. "Break up? What for?"

"They think we're too young to be spending so much time together. They think we should be 'free' our senior year to meet new people. They think we might be getting too serious about each other." Lexi gave a helpless little shrug. "I don't know. Maybe they think we'll get into the same kind of mess Peggy and Chad got themselves in."

Todd snorted sarcastically. "We're not Peggy and Chad. Besides, I don't want to be 'free.' There's no other girl at Cedar River High that I'd even want to date!"

"And no guy for me. I tried to tell them, but they wouldn't listen. They said it would be bad parenting if they didn't step in and make their wishes known."

Anger flashed in Todd's eyes. "But it's *our* lives."

"I know."

"Then why do you sound like you are resigned to go along with them?" His fingers squeezed tightly around hers.

"I wasn't. I hate what they're asking, but I don't have a choice."

"They're *making* you do this?"

"Not exactly." Then Lexi quoted the verses she'd found in the Bible. "If I say I'm a Christian, then I don't have much choice but to honor my parents. They have my best interests at heart."

"You don't sound so sure."

"I don't want to obey them, Todd. I don't want things to change between us, but they are my parents. . . ." The tears returned full force, and Lexi wept, her face buried in Todd's shoulder.

"They can separate us, Lexi, but they can't make us stop being friends," he said softly, stroking her hair.

She looked at him through a teary gaze. "So . . . you don't mind?"

"Mind? It makes me furious!" He paused. "But my parents have been saying the same sort of junk about being too 'tied down' and 'too young.'"

"Why didn't you say something?"

"Because I couldn't. I don't want us to be apart, Lexi." His expression was grim. "I've never known a girl like you, and I don't want our parents to mess things up. They don't understand our relationship. They don't realize that we're . . ."

". . . friends first . . ."

". . . and dating second."

"Or that we can read each other's minds . . ."

". . . and finish each other's sentences."

Lexi choked on a sob. "Oh, Todd, what are we going to do?"

He put his head back on the seat and sighed. "I don't know. Mom and Dad are usually pretty cool about things. They were even cool when my brother's fiancée found out she had AIDS. That must mean they feel pretty strongly about this."

"I know. Mine too."

"It's just so unreasonable. They don't get it!" Todd sounded angry and frustrated.

"Maybe we'll have to prove ourselves to them," Lexi ventured unhappily.

"What do you mean?" Todd sounded anxious.

"I don't know exactly. Talk to them. Agree to do what they ask for a while to show them that we aren't just foolish teenagers."

"How long?" Todd obviously didn't like what Lexi was saying.

"A month? Two? I don't know. How long would they say? I couldn't bear it if they wanted us to stay apart the whole year."

"I think they believe that if we quit seeing each other exclusively we'll find others to date and lose interest in our relationship," Todd said bluntly.

"But that won't happen!" Lexi wailed. "Will it?"

"Of course not."

"I'm scared, Todd. Really scared." Her voice was soft and quavery.

"So am I, but if we're supposed to be together, then we will be, right?"

"My parents said the same thing," Lexi admitted. "But this doesn't feel good. I don't think I can stand seeing you out with other girls—and there's not another guy in the world I'd want to date."

An impish grin slid across Todd's face. "I could ask Binky out and you could go with Egg."

"That would make Harry and Angela really happy."

"Just kidding. But don't worry, Lexi. There'll never be another girl but you."

"I hate this, Todd. We're talking about breaking up!"

"For a month or two. Then we'll talk to our parents about it. If we're reasonable, they will be, too. They want us to spread our wings, that's all. If they know we're adult enough to try it, that might prove we've got our heads on right and they don't have to worry about us."

"But what if that's not what happens?" Lexi was already feeling an emptiness growing inside her. She looked up at Todd and saw tears in his eyes.

"I don't know, Lexi. I just don't know."

Chapter Four

It was the most grim slumber party she'd ever attended, Lexi thought gloomily. Peggy, who'd invited them all to her place, was as nervous as a mouse at a cat convention. Lexi knew she was planning to tell Binky tonight about her family's upcoming move. Binky was already grouchy, a quality she'd been quick to exhibit lately. Anna Marie and Angela had been unable to come.

That left only Jennifer, who was freaking over an upcoming English lit test she wasn't prepared for. Being dyslexic, Jennifer was always behind in her studies, and reading gave her the most trouble of all.

Even the food wasn't being eaten. Mrs. Madison had baked homemade pizzas, which were untouched on the counter—except for one piece that Binky had taken and pulled apart until strings of mozzarella were littered like tiny white snakes all over the plate.

From the corner of her eye, Lexi saw Peggy pick up a sheet of paper, draw a deep breath, and clear her throat. "I have something I'd like to ask all of you. Lexi and I have talked about this, but I want my other friends' opinions, too.

"I've found a bulletin board on the Web that allows mothers to send messages to babies they've given up. Should I try it?"

Peggy had everyone's attention now.

Binky looked puzzled. "What good would it do? Your baby isn't old enough to read!"

"It's for the adoptive parents, silly!" Jennifer howled.

"Oh." Binky went back to stretching a piece of cheese until it snapped. "Whatever."

"That's all you can say?" Peggy gasped. " 'Whatever'?"

"I'm sorry. I just have a lot on my mind, that's all." Binky still sounded more focused on herself than on Peggy.

"Peggy does, too," Lexi said softly.

"I'd wait a few years. Maybe your child will start looking for you," Jennifer suggested.

"But once my address changes—" Peggy stopped midsentence and put her hand over her mouth, but it was too late. Binky had already picked up on the slip.

"What do you mean, 'once my address changes'? Your address had better *not* change!" Binky sounded panicked.

"I didn't mean to let it slip out like that," Peggy murmured. "I wanted to tell you differently. . . ."

"Tell us what?" Binky asked.

"That my family is moving at the end of the school year."

"Nooooo!" Binky's protest was half cry, half howl. "You can't. No one else can move. I won't let them!"

"Dad got a great job, and he can't turn it down. It'll be all right, Binky. We can write to each other, email, call . . ."

Binky stood up and began to stomp around the kitchen, swinging her arms and shaking her head. "Everything is changing too fast. If Egg goes and you go, Peggy, who'll be left?"

"Thanks a bunch," Jennifer retorted.

"Yeah," Lexi added.

"You know what I mean." Then she turned to where Lexi and Jennifer were sitting. "Or maybe you don't. You aren't losing a brother *and* a friend!"

Much to everyone's shock and surprise, Lexi suddenly burst into tears.

In an instant, the other girls were hovering over her anxiously, rubbing her shoulders and murmuring soothing words.

"I didn't mean to sound so selfish, Lexi," Binky said contritely. "I know I've been thinking about myself a lot lately. I'm sorry."

"It's not you," Lexi choked. "It's . . ." She couldn't continue.

"And I don't *want* to move." Peggy was nearly in tears, too. "But I don't have any choice."

"Don't cry, Lexi. You're the one who always has

the answers." There was near panic in Jennifer's voice. "Things must be really bad if *you* are crying!"

It took Lexi a few moments to get ahold of her emotions. "It's okay. I didn't mean to bawl like a baby. I just . . ."

"We've all been feeling sorry for ourselves," Jennifer said firmly. "And we've totally ignored how *you* have been. What's up, Lexi?"

The threesome stared at her expectantly, their own problems forgotten now that they realized their friend was obviously in trouble.

"My parents are making me break up with Todd."

Stunned silence filled the room as the girls tried to process Lexi's statement.

"Break up?" Binky was the first to speak. "You *can't* break up! You and Todd are perfect together."

"Practically an institution or something," Peggy added. "Poster teens for perfection. Like Barbie and Ken."

"What are your parents thinking?" Jennifer huffed. "That would be a disaster!"

"They're thinking of me. And of Todd. They don't want us to be so exclusive. They don't think it's healthy. They want us both to date other people."

"Sick." Binky sat down on the bed and crossed her arms. "What goes on in parents' minds anyway?"

"Todd's parents feel the same way. They don't

want us to get too serious and have problems like . . ." Lexi stopped speaking.

"Like Chad and I did?" Tears came to Peggy's eyes. "You aren't as stupid as I was, Lexi. And you have God in your life. I didn't—not like I do now. What happened between us then—two dumb teenagers having sex—would never happen now. Never ever. I know now why God wants us to save that for marriage. It can only cause pain and problems when you do things outside His will."

"I think they know we're smarter than that. And that we're best friends. They just want to make sure we experience a good senior year."

"But that would be *with* Todd, not without him," Jennifer pointed out.

"I know that. You know that. But my parents aren't so sure. I know they aren't trying to hurt me . . ." Lexi's face crumpled. "But it hurts anyway."

"What does Todd say about this?"

"He's no happier than I am, but his parents have been saying the same thing."

"So don't listen to them," Binky suggested angrily.

"I thought of that," Lexi admitted before going on to explain what had happened when she'd turned to her Bible for help. "I just can't disobey them."

"Maybe you and Todd can show them how reliable and *un*foolish you are and they'll relent," Jennifer suggested.

"That's what we're hoping." Lexi sighed miserably. "I just can't believe how everything is turning out."

"Me, neither, and I'm getting mad!" Binky's hair was practically standing on end, and the spark in her eyes was one of fury. She tilted her head upward until she appeared to be looking right through the ceiling. "All right, God. What are you doing up there anyway? Why are you letting all this happen to us? We were happy and now we're a mess. I don't get it!"

"How do you know *God* is doing this?" Jennifer asked.

"I don't. But I know He could put everything right if He wanted to." Binky scowled and crossed her thin arms over her chest. "And I'm not going back to church until He does."

"Binky!" Jennifer yelped. "Are you trying to *threaten* God? That's worse than dishonoring your parents!"

Binky's stern expression wavered and her shoulders sagged. "Okay, maybe that's not such a good idea . . . but I'm still mad. I feel let down. Like God's not a friend of mine anymore."

Lexi had been listening to this exchange thoughtfully. Finally she spoke. "God always answers prayer, you know."

"Hah!" Binky sputtered. "He hasn't been answering mine."

"You don't know that."

"What do you mean?"

"God answers our prayers, but sometimes the answer is no," Lexi explained.

Binky blinked, startled.

"I know He wants what's best for us—even if we think that something else is better at the moment. He sees the whole picture. Maybe we should start trusting Him a little more instead of getting mad at Him."

Binky slumped onto a chair. "God's the big-picture guy, huh? I suppose that makes sense, His being omnipotent and all. But I still don't see why you and Todd have to break up."

"I don't, either," Lexi said with a sigh. "But I don't know how to stop it."

———

Lexi had been moping around the house all evening. Even Ben hadn't been able to get her to play a game of checkers. She'd tried to study, but the words just didn't sink in. She'd tried to sew but cut a hole right in the middle of the skirt she was making and couldn't repair it until she got to the store for more fabric. She'd taken a long, hot bath, done her nails, and now she lay on the living room floor, staring at the ceiling.

Through it all, her parents had said nothing, obviously knowing what was wrong and not being willing to back off of the stand they had taken.

Lexi flinched when the phone rang. She hoped it wasn't for her. She didn't want to talk to anyone unless it was Todd.

And it was not likely to be him. Word was out at school that they weren't dating anymore, and the Hi-Fives had been all over him during lunch hour. It had made Lexi so sick she'd had to leave, her food uneaten. At this very moment, Minda Hannaford was probably talking his ear off on the phone, trying to get him to come to some party or another—one that Lexi wouldn't be invited to.

"Lexi, it's for you." Ben carried the cordless phone into the living room and handed it to his sister. "A boy."

"Todd?" Lexi mouthed.

Ben shook his head. "Don't think so."

"Hello." Lexi's voice was less than welcoming.

"Hello yourself. You sound like you're in a lousy mood."

"Jerry? Is that you?"

"Who else?"

"Why are you calling?"

He whistled into the phone. "Don't be so friendly or I might change my mind and hang up."

"Sorry. It's been a bad week." Lexi glanced at her father, who was pretending to read the paper.

"So I heard. Sorry about Todd and the parents thing."

"Me too."

Jerry was quick. "Are your parents in the room?"

"You've got it."

"Then what I've got to say might make them happy."

Puzzled, Lexi asked, "What do you mean?"

"I just figured that since I was the first guy who ever asked you out when you moved to Cedar River, it would only be appropriate to be the first guy to ask you out now, too."

"You're kidding, right?"

"No. There's a big concert in the park on Sunday night. New bands that are supposed to be really cool. Wanna go?"

Lexi had heard about the "Battle of the Bands." She and Todd had even talked about going before . . .

"That's really sweet of you, Jerry, but I don't think . . ." Then Lexi noticed her father glance up from the paper, an interested expression on his face. Jennifer's comment came back to her. *"Maybe you and Todd can show them how reliable and unfoolish you are and they'll relent."*

"Well, I guess the Battle of the Bands would be fun to go to—just as friends, of course."

"Of course," Jerry said insincerely. "It's a date, then?"

"No, not a date. But I'll go with you because I want to hear the music."

"All right. I'll pick you up at seven. Wear a jacket. They're going to play late and it might get cold. I'll bring a couple lawn chairs or camp stools or something."

"Fine," Lexi said absently, already feeling as if she'd betrayed Todd. But when she hung up and turned to look at her father, the expression on his face was one of approval. With a sinking heart, Lexi knew that she'd done the right thing for her parents, if not for herself.

———————

"You look great!" Jerry's words of admiration did nothing to bolster Lexi's mood. She didn't feel great, and she certainly hadn't meant to look special for this evening. She'd pulled her hair off her face in a severe ponytail and put on an old plum-colored sweater and faded jeans. But apparently that was exactly the right attire for the Battle of the Bands. Jerry, who was usually very particular about his clothing, was similarly dressed.

Lexi silently slipped into the car after Jerry gallantly opened the door for her. She'd never felt so miserably out of place in her entire life. It should be *Todd's* car she was sitting in and *Todd* climbing behind the wheel.

"Weird, huh?" Jerry said.

Lexi looked at him sharply. "What?"

"I was just remembering our first date—right after you moved to Cedar River. And now we're having a first date again."

She flinched. "Listen, Jerry, this isn't really a date."

"And I'm not really a guy," Jerry said with a smirk. "Come on, Lexi, accept it. Everyone in school knows you and Todd can't see each other because your parents said you couldn't. You either are dating or you aren't. The way I see it, this is a date." Then he gave her a sympathetic look. "I've grown up a lot since we were sophomores. I was a pretty crude, egotistical guy back then. I hope now we can be friends."

Lexi slumped farther down into the seat. "Of course. We *are* friends. I probably should be grateful to you that you are the one who asked me out. I feel so wretched that I wouldn't want to go to the concert with anyone but a good friend."

"Great." There was satisfaction in Jerry's voice. "Now just relax and have some fun."

She almost did relax during the ride to the park. Jerry talked about trivial things that had happened at school and crazy things that went on at the Hamburger Shack, where he worked, obviously trying to put Lexi at ease. Still, it was hard not to be with Todd, who was so familiar and so comfortable that sometimes they just rode together in silence, practically knowing what the other was thinking.

Jerry whistled softly. "I didn't expect it to be this full."

Lexi realized for the first time that makeshift parking lots had been set up all around. People, mostly teens, were streaming into the park in droves. Lexi recognized some from Cedar River High, but most of them were strangers.

"I didn't realize this would be such a big deal," she commented.

"You haven't been reading the paper or listening to the radio, then," Jerry said. "It's been advertised for days."

"I guess I haven't been paying much attention to anything," Lexi admitted. "I've been in a fog."

Jerry grinned. "Then it's time to let some sunshine in."

Lexi was surprised at how nice Jerry could be. He seemed to genuinely understand how sad she'd been and was doing everything in his power to cheer her up. She'd underestimated him, she decided. He deserved better than the mopey person she'd become. She made a decision to be at least a pleasant companion for the evening.

"There are the Hi-Fives!" Lexi pointed out. "What has Rita done to her hair?"

"Something with blue paint," Jerry observed. "Who knows with her?"

"It *is* weird. When I moved to Cedar River, I had so much trouble with those girls. Now it's as if we've learned to agree to disagree. They're still annoying, but we don't have the problems we once did."

"My aunt calls that growing up. She says even *I'm* doing it." Jerry turned to Lexi with a wide, charming smile. "No one in my family ever thought it would happen."

Lexi burst out laughing. Her heart lightened just a little.

Jerry found a parking place not too far from the band shell, and together they carried their lightweight lawn chairs and two lap robes to an empty spot on the quickly filling lawn. Jerry set up the chairs and even tucked the blanket around Lexi's knees before asking her if she'd like something from the concessions stand.

"That sounds great." Lexi's appetite had been nonexistent, but suddenly she was feeling very hungry. "I'll have a hot dog and a soda."

"Coming up." Jerry dodged his way through the crowd, leaving Lexi to study the scores of people waiting for the concert to start.

She saw Tim Anders in the audience with a girl she didn't know. Matt Windsor waved at her as he passed with a group of his friends. Anna Marie and Peggy stopped to say hi and to offer Lexi some of their stash of red licorice before moving on to a spot on the grass a few yards away.

Lexi had always loved to watch people, and this was the perfect opportunity. God had really created a variety in humanity, she thought, and He loved everyone exactly the same. It was a comforting thought.

She was feeling better than she had in days when she spied a couple setting up camp chairs several feet in front of her. The thick gold shock of hair and wide shoulders of the young man were achingly familiar. Todd. But Lexi did not recognize the girl he was with. She had jet black hair that hung past her shoulders, smooth, creamy skin, and a smile that dazzled as she turned it toward Todd. She was breathtakingly beautiful.

A knife turned in Lexi's heart.

God might love everyone just as they were, but Todd was human, and there was no way Lexi could compete with a girl who looked like that.

He hadn't waited long to find another date, Lexi thought sourly even as she realized that she had done the same by going out with Jerry.

But there was no way Todd could be jealous of *Jerry*. On the other hand, the beautiful creature Todd was escorting . . .

By the time Jerry returned with the food, Lexi felt as though her world had crumbled. It was all she could do to pretend that she was enjoying the rest of the evening. Jerry deserved that much.

Laughing on the outside, crying on the inside. Now Lexi knew exactly what that old cliché meant.

———

"I think life is a total bummer," Binky announced. She and Lexi were commiserating at Lexi's house the day after the concert. "Nothing is fair. Egg's leaving. Peggy's moving. Now Todd and this hot new girl who no one knows. You with a broken heart. Life's gross."

"It's going to work out," Lexi said. "It has to. The Bible says that *all* things work together for those who love God."

"Sure, but *when*?"

Lexi didn't want to discuss it anymore and was relieved when Ben entered the room. He'd just showered, and his dark hair was combed away from his face. With a start, Lexi realized how grown-up he looked.

"What's up, Ben?" Binky asked.

"I'm going bowling."

"Bowling?" Lexi was surprised. "With who?"

"The academy has started a new program," Lexi's mom said as she walked up behind Ben and put a hand on his shoulder. "It's to prepare the youngsters for the day they'll graduate and go into group homes."

"But that's not for a long time yet!" Lexi protested.

"Time passes quickly, Lexi. After all, we've already lived in Cedar River two years. The program introduces the academy's students to group home residents and caretakers. It's just a taste of independence and fun, that's all." Mrs. Leighton gave Ben a hug. "He's not going anywhere for a while."

Ben wrinkled his nose at the gooey display of affection but allowed his mother the luxury. Then the doorbell rang, and a young man from the group home came to pick up Ben.

When he'd left and Mrs. Leighton had returned to her artist's studio, Lexi flopped down on the couch with a groan. "I'm in no better shape than you, Binky. My brother's leaving, too!"

"Just for the afternoon, silly."

"Today that's true. But he's growing up. He's a pretty cool little dude even if he does have Down's syndrome. He's not going to stay my baby brother forever."

Binky sighed. "I know how you feel."

The two girls sat morosely on the couch staring at the floor, shoulders drooping, their worlds crashing down around them.

Chapter Five

"Hi, Lexi," Peggy greeted as she stepped into the Leighton house. Binky and Jennifer were already in the kitchen halfheartedly making cookies. Jennifer was rolling the dough into balls and squashing them onto a cookie sheet while Binky spent most of her time eating the dough right out of the bowl.

"It's good you came when you did," Lexi whispered. "Binky might have eaten all the dough before we got a dozen cookies."

"I'm not hungry, thanks."

"Me, neither, but we thought we'd better find *something* to do. We're all bored out of our minds tonight. No homework. No dates."

"No nothing!" Binky added. "Unless you have something great to tell us."

"Hardly." Peggy sat down on an empty stool near the counter. "I was coming here to get cheered up."

"You called that one wrong," Jennifer muttered.

"What's the trouble?" Lexi asked, immediately concerned for her friend.

"I had a long talk with my parents. They think I should wait to start looking for my baby's adoptive parents. It's a long shot anyway, and chances of seeing my baby are probably better if she looks for me someday."

"How do you feel about that?" Lexi wondered.

Peggy shrugged. "Sad. Relieved. Confused. I guess my parents are right. I just want to know that someday I'll have the opportunity to talk to my child."

She eyed the other girls sternly. "Don't *ever* get into the mess I did. There's so much pain. . . ."

"You don't need to tell us," Jennifer said. "We've watched you suffer. Besides, it's Saturday night and we're all here—dateless and baking cookies! None of us appear to be in any danger of a serious relationship." She paused and glanced across the table. "Sorry, Lexi."

Lexi didn't speak. The visual of Todd and the gorgeous dark-haired girl at the concert had been eating at her for almost twenty-four hours now, and still the pain hadn't abated.

Honor your father and your mother. She'd never dreamed that would be such a difficult thing to do.

———

Lexi hadn't imagined, either, the gossip that would be swirling around the school on Monday morning after everyone had seen her with Jerry, and Todd with the still-unidentified girl.

In every class someone, usually a Hi-Five, brought it up. Lexi, devastated, refused to respond. It was bad enough that she and Todd were apart but worse that he'd found someone so beautiful so quickly.

What's more, Todd seemed to be avoiding all the places that they used to meet—the lunchroom, at their lockers, by the doors after school. He even avoided the *Cedar River Review* work room, where the school paper was put together. It was as though he'd dropped out of school entirely.

She was not the only one to notice.

Egg meandered up to her in the hallway after school and asked, "Have you seen Todd? He promised to let me use his notes for a makeup test I have to take. I haven't seen him all day."

"I haven't, either."

"*I* have." Minda's voice sang out with false sweetness. "He just left the building through the back door. On the way to see his new girlfriend, no doubt."

"You don't know that," Egg rebutted.

"Don't I?" Minda gave him a pitying glance. "McNaughton, you're so out of it."

"And you're so 'in.' Who's the girl, anyway?"

Minda hesitated to glance at Lexi. "She's from the private school on the other side of town. I don't know her name, but I do know she's going to be a varsity cheerleader next year. I saw her at cheer-leading camp."

Lexi felt as if she'd been hit in the stomach. She'd practically forgotten that the private school existed. It was very small and elite and the students rarely mixed with those from the public school. *"Too rich,"* Todd had always said.

Apparently he'd changed his tune.

She had to escape. With a murmured good-bye to Egg and Minda, Lexi headed for the closest exit. She needed to be alone to have a conversation with the One she'd always considered her dearest friend.

As soon as she was out of sight of the school, Lexi began to pray out loud as she walked. For a long time, the conversation seemed very one-sided.

"I don't get it, God. I'm doing what you asked me to do! I'm obeying my parents, and look where it's gotten me! Todd already has a new girlfriend, we're the gossip of the whole school, and I'm miserable!"

Tears came to her eyes, and she let them slide down her cheeks. "I miss him, God. And I don't see the point in us being apart. We're responsible people, and it's no fun being 'free' like my parents said it would be. I'm just lonely."

As she walked and prayed, a calmness started to settle around Lexi. Her breath slowed and her footsteps became less frantic. She finally quit talking and started to listen.

It was as if a voice deep within her was saying, *It will be all right. Trust me.*

Lexi stopped right in the middle of the sidewalk, nearly tripping an elderly lady walking her dog. *Trust Him.*

That was the very thing she *hadn't* been doing—trusting God. She'd taken all this worry upon herself and grown miserable in the process. That was fruitless because Lexi knew she had to do what her parents asked. All she could do was trust God to work things out.

As she stood there, she realized that she felt as if a weight had been lifted from her shoulders. Nothing had changed, really. She and Todd were still seeing other people. But now she'd turned her unhappiness and frustration over to God, who, amazing as it was, *wanted* her to do just that.

"Okay, Lord, if you insist," she said. "You can worry about my problems from now on. They're all in your hands now."

Lexi began to walk toward home again, realizing that she hadn't felt this good since before she had "the talk" with her parents about her relationship with Todd.

"You'll never guess who just called me!" Lexi met Jennifer at the door. "I still can't believe it!"

"Who? Who?"

"Chris Corbin!" exclaimed Lexi.

"Who's that?"

"Don't you pay any attention to our football team? He's the quarterback!"

"The big guy with all the muscles and the really short haircut? What did he want?"

"To ask me out."

Now she had Jennifer's interest.

"Are you kidding? Minda would spit nails if she knew that! She's been trying to get a date with him for forever. What did he say?"

"Just that he'd heard Todd and I weren't seeing each other for a while and that he had wanted to take me to a movie!" Lexi couldn't help feeling excited. Her self-confidence had taken a downward turn lately, and attention from the high school's biggest jock didn't hurt.

"Are you going?"

"Yes."

"When?"

"Tomorrow night."

Jennifer exhaled. "Wow. What are you going to wear?"

"I have no idea. Come upstairs with me and help me pick something out."

Jennifer's choice turned out to be a short ivory sweater set, dark brown jeans, and the new brown boots Lexi had just purchased at the mall.

"All you need with that is a gold chain. You're gorgeous!" she approved as Lexi raced around her bedroom frantically looking for the perfect jewelry.

"Lexi, you're a nervous wreck."

"This isn't like going out with an old friend, Jen. This is a guy I hardly know except from the write-ups in the *Review*. He's a legend at Cedar River High. I think I've spoken to him twice. What will I say?"

"You? Asking me? Just be yourself, Lexi. That's who he expects, you know."

"I know, but it's been so long since I've had to make conversation with someone I hardly know, besides the fact that we'll be on an actual date."

"Oh, Lexi, you'll be just fine."

———

The doorbell rang, and Lexi said a silent prayer for calmness, walked down the stairs, and opened the door.

Chris so fully filled the doorway that Lexi couldn't even see around him. She'd never been quite so close to him, and she'd forgotten how big he was.

"Come in," she finally murmured. She could feel her dad's eyes on her. He was in the living room, supposedly reading the paper but really waiting for an introduction.

"Sure, why not?" Chris moved forward, and Lexi melted backward out of his way. It was no wonder he was so good on the football field. Lexi felt a little like running away from him herself.

As she made the introductions, she could feel approval radiating from her father. She knew it was because she was doing as he had asked—

meeting others, being involved with more than her usual group of friends—but she wasn't particularly happy. In fact, the thought uppermost in her mind was of Todd. Was he taking the dark-haired girl out tonight, too?

Once in Chris's car, Lexi tried to take a full breath.

"What movie do you want to see?" He listed all those playing around town. Lexi picked one she'd heard was good. He nodded, shrugged, and put the car into gear.

Not a big talker, Lexi decided.

————

They'd had burgers at a drive-in, cruised the streets listening to music until it was time for the movie, then purchased huge bags of buttered popcorn and entered the theater just as the previews rolled. They'd hardly spoken three words to each other.

It was a comedy, and Chris laughed at jokes Lexi didn't think were funny at all, meanwhile devouring his popcorn and most of hers. Then he settled back for the rest of the movie.

But it obviously wasn't movie watching Chris was interested in, Lexi discovered when he slipped his arm around her shoulders. His arms were so big and strong, she felt like she was in a vise. Soon he was running his finger up and down her neck, over her shoulder and down her arm.

Eyes on the screen, Lexi gritted her teeth and

stared straight ahead. They'd hardly even spoken to each other. What made him think he had any right to touch her?

When she felt his other hand slip around her and his breath on her cheek, she wriggled out of his grasp.

He gave a grunt of disgust and pulled away.

There was even *less* to talk about on the way home.

When Chris pulled up in front of Lexi's house, she turned to face him. "I didn't mean to make things uncomfortable. Please don't take what happened earlier as an insult. . . ."

"Hey, forget it, okay. No big deal. You've been hanging around with Todd for a long time, so I just figured—"

"Well, you 'figured' wrong." Lexi kept a tight rein on her temper. "Good night, Chris."

"Yeah. Whatever."

This time Lexi opened the car door herself. It was obvious Chris had no intention of trying to be a gentleman anymore. She got out, slammed the car door, and watched his taillights disappear before turning toward the house. *This* was supposed to be a better experience than being with Todd? No way.

Chapter Six

"It should be at the Hamburger Shack," Jennifer insisted. "We all have good memories of that place."

"Are you sure you wouldn't rather have it at someone's house?" Anna Marie asked. "More private and all."

"I know!" Binky chirped. "Let's get Jerry to help us plan. Maybe he can ask his boss if we can get the Shack after hours and have a private party there."

"Good idea," Jennifer approved. "Jerry can also plan our menu—maybe he can get us a good deal on burgers or pizza or something."

"And he'll have to ask if we can decorate," Angela added.

Lexi was silent throughout the conversation about Peggy's going-away party. Usually she was one of the most energetic of party planners, but lately her enthusiasm for everything had taken a nose dive.

"Sounds to me as though we can't go any further until we talk to Jerry. Lexi, could you call him and see when we can get together?"

Lexi's head jerked at the sound of her name. "Why me?"

"You see more of him than the rest of us do," Jennifer reminded her. "Remember?"

"Hardly."

"The Battle of the Bands? Bowling? The walk for charity? Weren't you together for all of that?"

"We're not dating. Jerry just asked me and I didn't have anything else to do!"

"No one *said* you were dating," Anna Marie commented. "But you *are* friends, and you *do* see more of him than the rest of us."

"Oh, all right," Lexi muttered. "But don't get any ideas. . . ."

The other girls exchanged glances. Lexi had been very sensitive lately. It was bad enough that she and Todd were staying apart, but the girl he was seeing was so incredibly beautiful that Lexi felt as though she didn't have a chance of regaining his interest.

Todd was practically invisible to everyone these days—coming to school late and leaving as soon as the final bell rang. He'd quit hanging out with Egg, Matt, and Tim. He wasn't even spending time at his brother's garage. It was as though he'd disappeared from the face of the earth. More likely, he'd disappeared into his new friend's living room.

Because he'd spent so little time with his

friends, no one knew much about either him or the girl. Even the Hi-Fives—who made it a practice to know all the gossip they could—didn't have much information. They were almost as frustrated by the situation as Lexi!

"Are we going to give her a going-away gift?" Angela asked, breaking into Lexi's reverie. "We could all chip in to buy something she could remember us by."

"She'd better not forget us!"

"Don't worry, Binky. You, especially, are unforgettable." Jennifer grinned wickedly. "Even if someone wanted to forget you, they couldn't. No how, no way."

Angela, ignoring the banter, continued. "She'll be spending her senior year in a strange high school with a class she doesn't know. What kind of gift would help her through that?"

"Stationery so she could write to us?"

"A phone card so she could call us?"

"An airline ticket so she could come for a visit?"

"A change in her dad's plans?" Binky said grumpily.

"You aren't any help at all," Jennifer chided.

"I don't care. I'm mad."

"You're always mad."

Patiently, Angela attempted to steer the discussion back to the gift. "I like the idea of a prepaid phone card, but we need to give her something more *permanent*, too."

"I've got it!" Jennifer said. "Let's get her one of

those really cool leather binders. She can use it for high school and for college. On the inside we can make a photo collage of all her friends and put it in a protective plastic sheet. Then every time she uses the binder she'll think of us 'cause there we'll be!"

Everyone digested the idea.

"I like it," Lexi said.

"Me too," Angela, Anna Marie, and Binky chimed.

"Great. Then we can all start looking for photos we want to include."

"And we can take new ones, too," Anna Marie said. "We can fill several pages if we want."

"I'll look for a binder," Jennifer offered. "There's a great stationery and office supply store at the mall. I'll find out what they cost and see who wants to go in on the gift."

"It's settled, then." Angela looked relieved. "Lexi will work with Jerry on the party, Jennifer will buy the gift, and we'll all work on the photos."

"Who's going to do the invitations?" Jennifer asked.

"I will," Anna Marie offered. "Just tell me who to include."

They began to rattle off names, and Anna Marie hurriedly scribbled each down on the back of her notebook.

"What about dates?" Jennifer asked. "Some of these people might want to bring someone else."

"No!" The exclamation slipped out of Lexi's

mouth unbidden. In her mind she could see Todd walking into the Hamburger Shack with the dark-haired girl on his arm. Even the thought made her want to curl up and cry. She couldn't handle it in person.

"He wouldn't be that dumb!" Jennifer blurted, reading Lexi's mind.

"No way." Binky looked furious. "If Todd did that to you . . ."

Lexi shook her head. "It's okay. It's not fair to make rules for everyone just so I won't be hurt. It's Peggy's party. We want it to be big and festive. We can't ask people not to bring friends."

"But what about—"

"I can take it." Lexi smiled weakly. "Maybe Jerry or Egg or Matt will ask me to go with them. At least that way I won't feel like such a loser."

"They'd all ask you and you know it," Jennifer said. "I still can't believe your parents did this to you. They've messed up everything!"

Lexi wiped away a tear. She'd been praying long and hard about this, and she still didn't understand why her life had taken this turn. All she knew was that if she were to live the faith she believed in, she had to obey her parents. She'd left God in charge, and He would make all things work for the good of His children.

———

"Jerry, you are amazing! This is the coolest party ever!" Peggy flung her arms around his neck and gave him a kiss on the cheek. Jerry flushed with pleasure and embarrassment, but Peggy's praise was well deserved.

Jerry had not only negotiated for the Hamburger Shack and a buffet of practically everything on the Shack's menu, including a huge cake emblazoned with WE LOVE YOU, PEGGY, but had also decorated the place himself with streamers and balloons. To top it off, he'd ordered a bouquet of daisies, Peggy's favorite flowers.

Lexi found Jerry in the kitchen about halfway through the party. He was loading the commercial dishwasher.

"Need help?"

He looked up. "You should be out enjoying the party."

"So should you."

"Nah. My boss said the only way he'd let me have the party here was if I made sure it was as clean as he'd left it. I thought I'd better get busy so I wasn't here all night. The gift was a big hit, wasn't it?"

"She loved it," Lexi agreed, "but don't try to change the subject. We'll all help you clean up. It's everyone's party. So far you've been stuck with all the work."

"I don't mind." Jerry leaned against the pristine stainless steel counter and wiped his hands on the front of his apron. "It feels good."

Lexi looked at him quizzically.

Jerry smiled sheepishly. "It's just that now,

with all of us facing Egg's graduation and Peggy's move, I feel like I should prove to everyone that I'm not a total jerk."

"Jerry! Why do you think like that?"

"Give me a break, Lexi. I haven't always been Mr. Nice Guy."

"You might have been a little . . ."

"Arrogant? Materialistic?" Jerry smiled wryly.

"You're so hard on yourself!"

"I call it honest. I've grown up a lot lately, Lexi. And I'd like to say thank you."

"For what?" This was the most amazing conversation she'd ever had with Jerry.

"For ever going out with me again after the way I treated you when you first came. I know it's just 'cause you and Todd can't see each other, but you could have said no."

"Jerry, I don't know what to say. . . ."

"Don't say anything." He kicked at the leg of the stove nearby. "I just wish that I'd been smart enough to see what a great girl you were back then. Of course, then it might have been you and me that your parents were trying to break up."

"We're all feeling a little melancholy, I guess. But it's a very sweet thing you just said. Thank you." Lexi felt tears sting at the backs of her eyes. Everything was so strange lately—strange and sweet and sad.

Suddenly the door to the kitchen burst open, and Binky stomped into the room with a look of utter disgust on her face.

"Do you have any whipped cream in here? No, that's too good for him. Rotten eggs maybe? Or something moldy?"

"My boss wouldn't allow spoiled food!" Jerry said indignantly. "And what do you want that for, anyway?"

"To dump on my brother. He's being more obnoxious and pompous than usual, that's all. He's dominating Peggy's party with his own big stories about how it's going to be at his school. Nobody can get a word in edgewise."

"I see," Jerry said sagely. "It's the Egg problem again. Why don't you just let him talk, Binky. He's excited about his future. There's nothing wrong with that."

"Yes, there is! I'll be left behind!"

"You have your own life, Binky. You'll be the senior next year," Lexi pointed out.

Binky sank onto a small stool and put her chin in her hands. "I'm not even sure what my life will be like without Egg."

Then, as if a light bulb sprang to life in Binky's head, she said, "Oh, I forgot to tell you. Todd was just here."

"Now? Is he outside?" Lexi's heart began to beat a little faster.

"No. He came to say hi to Peggy, then took off. He hardly talked to anyone."

"Oh." Lexi felt confused and disappointed. He didn't even *try* to find her.

"I told Tim it wasn't a good idea, but he told

Todd you were in here with Jerry. Do you think that's why he left so quickly?"

Lexi blanched. Both Jerry and Binky stared at her.

"Are you all right?" Jerry put a hand out to steady her.

"Did . . . did he have . . . *her* . . . with him?"

"He was alone, Lexi. I really don't think you have anything to worry about. Just because Todd's been seen out with this girl doesn't mean—"

"I don't have any business caring. We promised our parents we'd date other people." Lexi turned to Jerry, her eyes brimming. "And it's not all bad. Jerry and I have gotten to know each other again. And he's turned into a really nice guy."

"But not Todd," Jerry said wistfully.

"Not Todd, but there's not one thing wrong with that." Lexi scrubbed at her eyes. "And I have one more favor to ask you. Could you drive me home? It will only take a few minutes and you can be right back. I don't feel like staying any longer. Tell Peggy, will you, Binky? I'll talk to her tomorrow."

———

Lexi lay on her bed staring at the ceiling. Even Ben hadn't been able to cheer her up over dinner. When her parents had invited her to go to a going-away party for Peggy's parents, Lexi had declined. It was easier to just lie there and mope.

She even considered ignoring the phone when

it rang, but finally she rolled over and picked up the receiver. "Hello?"

"Lexi, hi."

"Todd?" She sat up, suddenly more energetic.

"Can you talk?"

"My parents are gone, if that's what you mean. But they wouldn't mind our talking anyway."

"About us."

Then Lexi understood. Butterflies whooshed about in her stomach. "What about 'us'?"

"I've missed you."

"I was in the kitchen during Peggy's party. You could have said hello."

"That was awkward. Besides, I didn't think we needed an audience."

"Jerry?"

"I hear you've been seeing a lot of him lately." Todd's voice was cautiously even.

"We're just friends. My life's been pretty boring lately. Not like yours." Lexi regretted the snide remark the moment it slipped through her lips. "I'm sorry. I didn't mean it like it sounded . . . it's just been so hard."

"You mean seeing me with Megan?"

Lexi felt herself grow cold inside.

"It's no big deal. We're just friends."

"You found new friends very quickly."

"Don't do this, Lexi," Todd pleaded. "I'm trying to talk to you, not argue."

"I'm sorry. I've just been in a terrible mood ever

since Peggy's party. I had no right to say that. We agreed . . ."

". . . to meet and see other people," Todd finished for her. "And I've met lots of nice ones, but none like you."

"Oh, Todd, that's exactly how I feel, but I don't know what to do about it. We promised our parents . . ."

"We don't have to *do* anything. I just wanted to let you know—in spite of my hanging out with Megan—that you are still the most special girl in the world. Actually, it's been kind of . . ." he searched for a word, "liberating."

"What?" That made no sense whatsoever to Lexi.

"It's not so scary. I know now that we can be apart and not *grow* apart. It's good to have lots of friends. I like that. We both know we can be apart if we have to—we just don't *want* to."

"I see what you mean." Lexi thought about the new friendship she and Jerry had developed. It wasn't romantic, but it was special. And she would have missed that opportunity if she were always hanging out with Todd.

"Together or apart, you're my best friend, Lexi. Our parents can't change that, and I don't think they'd want to. They're just obsessing about our ages, not our friendship. I'll bet if we were five years older, they'd think it was great that we were dating."

"Is that why you called? To tell me this?"

"Yes. And to tell you that I miss you. And to tell you things will work out. I know they will."

When Lexi hung up the phone, she was smiling softly. And even though Megan was gorgeous, Todd still liked her, Lexi, best. What's more, he thought things would work out.

Lexi felt practically lighthearted as she got ready for bed.

She picked up her Bible and thumbed through it until she came to the commandments she was looking for. *Honor your father and your mother*. It was one of the "Big Ten," as Pastor Lake would say. "Rules to build a life around."

Though she couldn't see the entire picture yet, a few things were coming into focus: Friendships were important to make and should not be ignored at the expense of a more romantic relationship; A guy could have not only a "girlfriend" but also friends who were girls; And, she should have *trusted* her parents as well as obeyed them.

Lexi had a long talk with God about the things she had learned and then slept that night better than she had in weeks.

Chapter Seven

"Are you going to youth group tomorrow night, Binky?"

Lexi and Binky were seated on the back steps of the McNaughton home, watching a red squirrel scamper through the large trees in the yard. More than once it looked as though he were about to fall, but he always managed to hang on and scramble to a stronger limb until he decided it was time to venture into dangerous territory again.

"No way."

"It sounds like you've really made up your mind," Lexi commented mildly, but in reality, she was surprised by Binky's emphatic answer.

"I don't want to go anywhere they're having a graduation party for the seniors in the group. I've had it up to here with them." Binky made a dramatic slash with her finger across her throat. "And my mom can't do anything but talk about the reception they're going to have here for Egg! Potato salad, ham on buns, Egg's favorite fruit salad—the kind with marshmallows and pudding—everything he likes to eat."

"Sounds nice to me. I hope we're invited."

"Oh, you will be. All of Egg's friends and their families are. I even had to help with the guest list!"

"And next year all this excitement will be over you."

"By then Mom and Dad will probably be so sick of Mr. Look-I'm-A-Graduate that they'll serve everyone cold cereal and tell them to go home early."

Lexi burst out laughing. "You are so funny!"

"Hilarious, I know." Binky kicked at a pebble on the step and sent it skipping into the grass.

"I think your sense of humor is coming back. Do I detect a slight bit of acceptance of big brother's graduation?"

Binky frowned. "I *have* been trying to think of reasons to be glad Egg is leaving."

"And?"

"So far I've come up with a few. There'll be no one to eat all the cereal and then put the empty box back in the cupboard. It drives me crazy when I get hungry for a certain cereal and find the box empty. Once he had *six* empty boxes in there!

"And his socks won't be smelling up the laundry hamper. Egg's socks smell like something died in them and—"

"I don't think I need to know any more about that," Lexi pleaded.

"And the messes he makes! Crumbs all over.

Pillows lost. TV remotes gone forever. Plus, he won't eat the crust on his toast. Sometimes he shoves his plates under the couch and then, by the time we find them . . ."

"It sounds to me like you should be celebrating, not moping. Now his college roommate will have to put up with all that."

Binky considered that for a moment. A small, satisfied smile crept across her features. "I never really thought about it that way before. And I'll get his bedroom! It's twice the size of mine. I'll have to paint it, of course. It's green now and wouldn't go with any of my things. Puke green, actually. Egg likes it, but who cares? He's the one bailing out. I wonder if he'd let me have his other furniture?"

Lexi sighed. Binky was like a pendulum, swinging from one extreme to the other. She hoped she hadn't done more harm than good with her pep talk about Egg leaving home.

———

Mrs. Waverly didn't even ask the class to be quiet as they pushed their way into the music room. She waited for the din to die down a bit before tapping a pencil on her music stand to get everyone's attention.

"I see you are all a bit restless today. Maybe we should start class by sharing with everyone all the news we have."

Silence descended on the room.

Mrs. Waverly chuckled. "I didn't mean to scare you. You don't have to share what you were talking about when you walked into the classroom. I want each of you to tell us what your plans are for the summer. Tim, let's start with you."

Tim Anders flushed at being singled out. "I've got a job with the park board. I'll be a T-ball coach for little kids."

"Good for you. Jerry?"

"The Hamburger Shack, of course. Sometimes I feel like I *live* there." He brightened. "But this summer my boss says I can be the night manager. If it works out, I can do it during the winter, too. It means a lot more cash if I can swing it."

"An advancement. Excellent. How about you, Minda?"

Minda looked smug. "I'm going to spend the summer with my cousin on Cape Cod." She ignored the whistles and snide remarks about coming back "snootier" than ever. "And both my parents are coming out to visit." Her face lit with pleasure. "We'll all be together there for a few days. We're going sailing on my aunt and uncle's boat!"

Mrs. Waverly smiled widely.

Lexi could practically read her teacher's mind. Minda's parents had had marital troubles for a long time, and Minda was obviously hoping for a reconciliation while they were out East. Lexi hoped so, too—for Minda's sake.

Mrs. Waverly went up and down the rows asking each student about their plans. It wasn't until she got to Binky that things became tense.

"I'm going to paint my brother's room. I've picked lilac because it will go with my comforter."

Egg nearly pitched forward out of his chair. "What do you mean you're going to paint your brother's room? What about your *brother*? There's no way he's going to sleep in a *purple* room!"

"You aren't even going to be in that room, Egg," Binky retorted. "I heard you tell Mom and Dad that you didn't think you'd be home until just before the fall semester. Besides, I have way too much junk for my little room. Yours is bigger. Could I use your bookshelves?"

Egg looked like he was being pumped full of helium. His cheeks were puffy and he was practically rising from his chair. "No, you may not use my shelves *or* my room!"

"If you want it, then stay home and use it," Binky said airily. "It's your choice, you know."

Egg sputtered and squirmed until he couldn't stay there anymore. He leaped to his feet, his long, gangly legs unfolding with a crack. "Mrs. Waverly, would you tell my sister that she's gone crazy? She's having separation anxiety, that's all. I've been here to take care of her all her life, and now I'm leaving and she's cracking up!"

"That's something the two of you should discuss," Mrs. Waverly said tactfully, "in *private*." Fortunately, she was used to Egg and Binky and their wacky relationship.

"You've been taking care of *me*? Who do you think has been taking care of *you*? Just wait, once you get to college, you'll be so homesick for me you'll be able to taste it! And I won't be there to get you out of the stupid jams you always get into. Why, you'll probably be calling home asking to come back to Cedar River within a week. And you can't have your room back—so there!"

Before Egg could retaliate, Mrs. Waverly said, "Binky, Egg, see me after class."

Egg shot his sister a now-look-what-you've-done glance and sat down. Binky smiled sweetly and nodded at Mrs. Waverly. It took Lexi everything in her power not to giggle.

———

"I can't believe we're actually packing your stuff!" Jennifer said, holding a pair of sneakers in front of her before dropping them into a carton marked SHOES.

"Me either," Peggy said. "I thought I'd be here forever—or at least through graduation." She held a framed photograph in her hand. "Remember Dmitri? The foreign exchange student from Greece?" She held out the picture for everyone to see. "I promised I'd write to him—often—and we've only exchanged a letter or two. I'm afraid that when we move I'm going to lose touch with all of you."

"Don't worry," Lexi said as she took clothes from Peggy's closet and hung them neatly in one of the mover-provided wardrobe boxes. "There are lots of us to write. We'll make a schedule to be sure you get at least one letter a week from Cedar River. How's that?"

"Only one?" Peggy tried to joke, but the words caught in her throat. She dropped the photo of her and Dmitri onto the bed and went to gather her friends in her arms.

They were all standing there in a huddle when the guys came trooping up the stairs to carry the first of the boxes to the main floor.

"What's this, a bawl-a-thon?" Tim asked.

"Don't bug us," Binky ordered. "We're having an important moment here."

"Why are you so concerned about Peggy moving and so suddenly unconcerned about me?" Egg asked grumpily. "Next thing I know, you'll have the movers picking up *my* stuff!"

Binky looked up, interested. "Good idea. When we finish here, we'll go to our place next. I really need the stuff out of your room before I can paint anyway. It would be good to get started right away. After all, graduation is this weekend."

Egg scowled, not sure if his sister was teasing or serious. But before he could challenge her, Todd and Matt each took one of his arms, turned him around, and sent him toward a pile of already filled boxes. Diverted for the moment, Egg sighed and began to work.

"This sure looks bare," Jennifer commented as

she took down the last of Peggy's posters and pictures.

"Horrible," Angela agreed. "I don't even recognize the place."

"And my parents already have a buyer for the house. A young couple with two small children. Kids just about the age I was when we moved here. Weird, huh?" Peggy moved a curtain aside to look at the growing pile of boxes on the front lawn.

"If houses could talk, they'd have a lot to say," Jennifer commented. "Especially the McNaughtons'."

Peggy burst out laughing. "Come on, let's drink some of that lemonade Mom made."

"And a few of the cookies Lexi brought over," Binky suggested.

"It's even getting empty down here," Jennifer commented from the main floor. Only the large pieces of furniture were left in each room.

"It's cheaper for us if we pack the little stuff," Peggy explained. "And we've given a lot of stuff away—outgrown clothes, toys, books, all sorts of stuff."

"Isn't that hard?" Angela asked.

"No. We gave it to a charity group that will distribute it to people in need. It felt kind of good, actually. I'm realizing more and more that material things don't count. Nice clothes, CDs, tapes, jewelry—all those things are fun to have, but they don't really matter. It's *people* that matter." Her expression softened. "People like you. Friends.

You can own all the 'stuff' in the world and still feel poor, but if you have good friends, you're rich no matter what."

Binky, her eyes moist, hugged Peggy. The other girls joined in just as Tim and Jerry walked into the room.

"Not *again*!" Tim said. "This is too much for me. Jerry and I ran out of things to do, so we're going to the mall. Anyone want to come?"

Lexi laughed. "I don't think so—especially not after what we were just talking about."

"What's that?"

"Material things versus the really important things in life."

Tim's eyes narrowed. "I think we'd better leave now, Jerry, or we'll be getting in on that touchy-feely-huggy stuff, too. See you later."

"What's left for us to do?" Angela asked.

"Not much. Mom's not going to clean until the movers have left. Since we're staying in a motel until after graduation, we'll have plenty of time for that."

Just then the rumbling of an engine caught their attention. A huge moving van was backing into the driveway.

"They're here!" Peggy gasped, turning pale. She sat down on a nearby chair with a thump.

"What's wrong? You look sick," Jennifer blurted.

"It just hit me. I'm moving. I really am moving." Tears began to stream down Peggy's face.

It was as though her tears were contagious. Next Binky started to cry, then Lexi, until everyone was sobbing.

"Why are we crying now?" Jennifer finally choked. "She's not even leaving till next Monday!"

"Because we can't help it," Binky retorted.

Lexi giggled at the strange conversation. Jennifer joined in. Soon they were laughing and crying at once.

Finally Peggy wiped away her tears. "Whew! I feel better now! I needed to get that out of my system." She smiled at her friends. "No matter where I go or what I do, I will never—ever—forget my friends in Cedar River. Now, let's take the guys to the mall. We don't have to actually buy anything. We need a break."

"Great idea," Jennifer said. "Lexi will drive."

"Oh, I will, will I?"

"Sure. You wouldn't want *me* driving, would you?"

"Okay, okay. Let's go."

They piled into Lexi's car, all eyes averted from the moving van in the driveway.

Chapter Eight

The day had actually arrived. Graduation. The old playground chant for the last day of school—"No more tests, no more books. No more teachers' dirty looks"—was a saying that probably held more meaning for Egg than for many of the other students. During his school years he'd generated plenty of "dirty looks" with his wild ideas and clumsy, puppylike enthusiasm.

But today he was different. He looked regal in his cap and gown, his skinny frame filled out with the billowing garment. The gold tassel on his mortarboard swung vigorously as he walked, and the grin on his face lit the hallways of Cedar River High.

Todd, Lexi, and Binky, among several others, had been chosen as junior class ushers. It was their responsibility to make sure the families of the graduating class were seated near the front of the gymnasium, to hand out programs, and then, when the time came, to march with the seniors down the wide aisle, escorting them to their reserved seats at the front of the auditorium.

The band was warming up in fitful starts and stops with an occasional eardrum-injuring squeak from the clarinet section. Conversation was buzzing at louder and louder volume as the room filled. People were beginning to use their programs for fans as the air became warm and heavy.

In the hallway, the seniors were getting restless. Lexi peeked around the corner trying to get a look at Egg.

He was intently studying the notes he'd written for his portion of the presentation. His face was somber. It struck Lexi that Egg looked more mature than she'd remembered. He had begun to fill out. The thin face was rounder, the Adam's apple less defined. When Lexi wasn't watching, Egg had grown up!

"We're ready," Mrs. Waverly whispered to Lexi. The first measures of "Pomp and Circumstance" were beginning in the auditorium. The group fell into place at the ushers' directions, and solemnly they began to march.

Binky held her head high as she performed her ushering duties, but tears streamed down her face.

She was not alone. As soon as the music burst forth full force and the graduating class began moving toward the podium, several people began dabbing at their eyes—especially in the family section.

A slide show was implemented to introduce

each of the seniors. The first photo was that of each student as an infant or young child. The second was a senior picture. The entire room burst into laughter at one of the photographs. It was of a long, skinny baby with spindly arms and legs, one leg bent so that the baby could suck on his toe. A startling shock of pale brown hair sprang from the baby's head, and though he was preoccupied with the sumptuous toe, his eyes were easily identifiable—Egg. The entire class began to applaud.

"Some things never change," Todd whispered to Lexi. "He's looked the same for eighteen years!"

The mood lightened and the ceremony continued with vocal and choral music and the long-awaited symposium speeches.

Egg, looking terrified, made his way to the podium, notes clutched in his hands. His voice crackled with nervousness as he began to speak.

"It . . . it's . . . scarier than I thought it would be up here," he stammered. Then Egg squinted at the crowd. "You all look smaller, too!"

When the laughter died down, Egg appeared more relaxed. "If there's anything I've learned here at Cedar River High, it's the importance of education, of relationships, of friends." He grinned. "That even includes teachers—you know who you are.

"Our class motto is 'Learn From Yesterday, Live In Today, Dream For Tomorrow.' I've been thinking about this for several days, wondering what it really means. Learning from yesterday?

What does that mean? Stay in line? Don't budge? Don't use all the paper towels in the guys' rest room to clean up a chemistry experiment? Bismarck is the capital of North Dakota? It had to be more than that. So I started to think about my yesterdays. About the time I was almost influenced to take steroids to bulk up because I was embarrassed to be the skinniest guy in the class. About the friend we all lost to suicide. About all I learned about the environment and what to do to keep it safe.

"It was then that I realized those were also the things I was *meant* to learn here—about life, about friendship, about being a good citizen of this planet. This school has been a microcosm of the bigger world, a place to get me ready for what comes next. When I realized that, *then* I knew what 'Learn From Yesterday' meant."

Lexi glanced at Peggy. She was weeping silently. Egg was really going for the jugular on this one. She hadn't realized what an eloquent speaker he could be.

"Then I turned to the second part of our motto, 'Live In Today.' That sounded pretty selfish at first, but the more I thought about it, the more I realized that living in today—in the moment—is all any of us *can* do. We can't change yesterday, and we don't know what tomorrow will be. All we can do is not waste time regretting things that happened yesterday, learn from our mistakes so we don't repeat them, and then move forward. Yesterday is over. Tomorrow isn't here yet. Don't waste the present rehashing the past.

"And those of you who know me well know I've made a few . . . well, goofy decisions." Egg blushed to the roots of his hair. "But I learned from them and let them go. I know now that every moment of life is precious—so enjoy it. Look for what is happy, beautiful, or funny in every moment of every day. What you believe will happen to you, most likely will.

"And that's why we should 'Dream For Tomorrow.' As we graduate, new doors open to all of us. Each of us has new goals toward which we can work. And because I know so many of you so well, I know that we all have the potential to accomplish whatever we set out to do. There's no guarantee that it will be easy, but don't let go of your goals. Sometimes things will go wrong. What is important is that *you* don't go wrong, too! After all, this graduating class and so many others just like us are the hope of tomorrow, the promise of what is yet to come."

Nearly everyone in the audience was dabbing at their eyes now. Mr. and Mrs. McNaughton were sitting so straight and tall in their chairs that Lexi thought they might just pop up and cheer, so proud were they of their sometimes geeky, suddenly awesome son.

"May God bless all of you in the future," Egg concluded. "Never forget how special you are. I'm proud to be a graduate of Cedar River High. I'd like to thank my friends for their loyalty and support and, most important, my family. Mom, Dad, Binky—I don't know what I'd have done without your love and support."

Egg sat down to a roaring round of applause. His face was as red as his mother's beet pickles, but he looked pleased with himself.

He should be. Lexi smiled through her tears. Egg had come through. She was so proud of him she thought she might burst.

The other speakers gave their speeches, but none so eloquently as Egg. There was more music from a seniorless version of the Emerald Tones and then the presentation of each senior and that exciting walk across the stage to pick up a diploma.

Egg, overly eager for this part of the ceremony, almost forgot to stop in front of the school official designated to move the seniors' tassels from one side of the mortarboard to the other.

"You're coming to my party, right? You'll be at my party? Don't forget my party!" Egg was busy shaking hands in the reception line and inviting everyone he knew to his home after graduation. "The food's going to be great. All my favorites and homemade buns for the ham. Don't miss it."

"Do you think his mother will have enough food for all the people he's inviting?" Jennifer whispered to Lexi.

"I guess we'll find out."

"That was the most beautiful graduation ceremony I've ever seen," Angela said. Her eyes were still puffy from crying.

"And next year it's us!" Anna Marie clapped her hands.

"I never thought I'd make it," Jennifer sighed.

"You haven't yet," Jerry pointed out jokingly. Then he held a protective hand over his face as if worried Jennifer might smack him.

"Ha-ha. Very funny. I've made it this far. There's no stopping me now!"

"Good! You can do it, just like Egg said you could!"

"Speaking of Egg, let's get over to his house."

———

Punch and food were flowing at the McNaughtons'. Binky had strung paper streamers from every light fixture and doorjamb. Helium-filled balloons bounced against the ceiling. Even the cat wore a big bow attached to its collar. Lexi had never seen it quite so festive at the McNaughtons'.

After collecting their food, everyone under the age of twenty gathered in Mr. McNaughton's small private den. The entire gang was there along with—amazingly—most of the Hi-Fives, including Minda, Rita, Gina, and Tressa. They all ate silently for a while before Rita broke the ice with a question.

"So how many of you are going to the senior party?"

"It's only for seniors, isn't it?" Anna Marie asked.

"Not *that* party, silly! I mean the *other* party. The one the kids plan and the parents know nothing about."

"Oh . . ."

"Where is it this year?" Matt asked. "I'm out of the loop."

"First time, I'll bet," Minda said slyly. "You used to be one of the first ones on the scene."

Matt shrugged. "I guess I've got other interests now."

"Anyway," Rita continued, "Egg has to make an appearance, don't you, Egg?"

Egg looked up from his potato salad. "Why?"

"Because you're a senior! It's what seniors do."

"I don't know. I've heard they can get pretty wild, those parties."

"Oh please!" Rita rose, and the other Hi-Fives did likewise. "We're going to the party right now."

"See you there?" Gina asked in a sugary tone.

After they'd left, the rest of the group glanced at one another. Matt was the first to speak. "It is a fun party—at least at first."

"What's that supposed to mean?" asked Binky, who'd been pretty sheltered from the party life.

Matt shrugged. "Go find out. See for yourself." He held out his hand. In it was a slip of paper. "Rita passed me a map to the spot."

"Egg, what do you think?" Lexi had almost forgotten Todd was in the room because he'd been so quiet and had been so good at making sure that he didn't sit anywhere near her. She wished her parents could see how well he was obeying their wishes! What made her miserable would have pleased them.

"I don't know. I suppose I could make an appearance—if you all come with me."

"It might be fun," Jennifer said.

"I'll go if everyone else does," Anna Marie added.

"Why not?" Egg made the decision for all of them. "It's my party and we'll go if I want to!"

"Are you sure about this?" Lexi whispered to Peggy. "I feel a little funny."

"It should be fine if we're all together. We can take more than one car. That way, if anyone wants to leave, it won't ruin things for everyone else."

For once, Lexi let herself be swept along by the crowd, but she did insist that she drive one of the cars. Egg and Todd drove the other two.

The party was being held at the end of a maze-like road outside of town.

"Are we lost?" Binky asked nervously as they followed Egg's taillights. Those were practically the first words Lexi had heard her utter since graduation. She'd been dazed and hollow eyed all afternoon.

"I see a bonfire," Peggy said. "See? Over there."

There were dozens of cars parked in a nearby

field and teenagers milling everywhere.

"Wow. I didn't expect it would be this big," Angela whispered. "And there are kids here I've never seen before."

"I think I know where they came from," Jennifer said, her voice grim. "The private school."

"What makes you think. . . ?"

There was no reason for Peggy to finish the question. A familiar face emerged from the crowd and headed straight for Todd. Megan.

Lexi felt her heart sink as she watched the dark-haired girl embrace Todd. Though he didn't return the hug, Lexi still felt as though she'd been kicked in the stomach. Then Megan said something to him and flashed a perfect smile his way. She took him by the arm and led him through the crowd until Lexi could no longer see where they had gone.

"We can leave right now," Binky said indignantly.

"It's okay," Lexi murmured. But it wasn't okay. It hurt.

Jerry slid an arm around her shoulders. "Let's walk up and look at the fire."

Lexi gratefully fell into step with him. "You've been a lifesaver, you know. I think I might have fallen into a heap right there."

"What are friends for?"

"Exactly. That's what I've realized most since my parents insisted Todd and I not see so much of each other. What I miss most is his friendship."

She glanced at Jerry. "The other thing I've realized is that I have a really good friend in you."

Jerry looked sheepish in the firelight. "Thanks, Lexi. I was a jerk for a long time. I guess I'm finally growing up."

She was going to respond, but laughter broke out on the far side of the fire. She could see teenagers passing something in a paper bag. Each in turn would put the bag to their lips and take a drink.

"Is that. . . ?"

"Liquor? Sure. That's the main reason everyone comes here—to drink." Jerry nodded toward a couple under the trees. "Or to make out."

Suddenly Lexi felt chilled. "I don't think I like this, Jerry."

"You don't have to take part."

"Just being here is taking part."

"Maybe. I thought you'd want to stay because of . . . well, you know."

"Todd and Megan? And what could I do about them? Watch her tug on his arm and smile at him? No thanks."

At that moment a guy, obviously drunk, staggered near the fire and lost his footing. Jerry and two others jumped forward and caught him just as he fell.

"Thanks, buddy," he mumbled.

"You could have been fried," Jerry said calmly. "You'd better stay away from the fire."

"Yeah. Thanks." The guy staggered off, oblivious to the tragedy that was just averted.

"*Now* I want to get out of here. Help me find Binky and the others to see if they want to stay or go."

The decision was unanimous among the girls. Everyone was ready to leave. They piled into Lexi's car, leaving Jerry behind to search out the other guys.

Lexi barely felt herself breathe until she turned onto the highway and sped toward home.

"I'm glad to be out of there!" Peggy said.

"What if the police had come?" Binky fussed. "I hope Jerry finds Egg and tells him to be sensible and leave."

"What about Todd, Matt, and Tim?" Peggy asked.

"They have brains. Here's their chance to use them." Jennifer was practical as usual.

"Do you think people will think we're all a bunch of 'goody-goodies?' " Binky wondered. "Leaving like that?"

"Do you really care?" Jennifer voiced Lexi's thoughts.

"No, I suppose not. It's just that sometimes I feel so . . . boring."

"That party looked boring to me. The only interesting thing I saw was that guy almost fall into the fire, and I know I can live without that kind of excitement." Peggy turned to look at her friends in the backseat of Lexi's car. "Actually, I'm very proud of us. We did the right thing."

"I hope Jerry gets the guys to do the right thing, too," Angela said.

Especially, Lexi added to herself, *Todd*. The image of him and Megan walking off together into the night was stuck in her head.

————

"Good morning to you! Good morning to you! Good morning, dear Lexi, good morning to you!"

Lexi opened her eyes to find Binky standing at the foot of her bed, singing at the top of her lungs. Lexi groaned and put a pillow over her head. She felt Binky jump onto the mattress.

"Wake up, sleepyhead! It's a beautiful day."

"Who wound you up this morning? What time is it?"

"Nine o'clock."

"On the third day of summer vacation? And you woke me up? Mom said I could sleep till noon all week!"

Then a thought occurred in Lexi's still sleep-muddled brain. "What's happened to you? Two days ago you were moping around, moaning and groaning about Egg leaving, and today . . ."

"It's so wonderful, I can't tell you, Lexi," Binky said with a delighted smile. "Egg refuses to get out of bed!"

"So do I. Now, go away."

"No, really. Like all day yesterday. My parents go to work and he just lays there."

That got Lexi's attention. "What's the matter? Is he sick?"

"No, he's not sick," Binky said, her tone indicating that Lexi was a bit thick not to understand immediately. "He's *miserable!*"

"And this makes you happy?"

"Of course it does."

Binky looked like she was being perfectly logical. However, McNaughton logic had very little to do with real-life logic.

"Why?"

"He's finally realized what a big step he's about to take. The morning after graduation, Mom woke him up and told him he'd better start packing 'cause they'd taken time off to drive him to college next week. After Mom left, Egg came into my room looking like he'd been hit in the head. He said he didn't want to go to school back East. That it was all a big mistake. That he wanted to stay near his family—especially *me*."

"So now Egg is regretting his decision?"

"Totally. He's really depressed."

"You shouldn't sound so happy about it," Lexi murmured. "Poor Egg."

"Don't you see?" Binky said impatiently. "Egg's being depressed is a sign that he really *does* appreciate me after all. Isn't that great?"

"So when Egg was happy, you were miserable. Now he's miserable, and you're happy. What's wrong with this picture?"

"Nothing. We're always like this. Egg will snap

out of it. He always does and so do I. Besides, I haven't told him my good news yet."

"What's that? That you burned all his suit-cases?"

"No, that my parents bought me a ticket to go out to visit him! He won't even have a chance to get lonesome and I'll be there. It will be so fun. We can take tours and go to museums and I'll get to see the campus. You know, I might like it so well that *I'll* want to go there, too! Wouldn't that be cool? Egg and I at the same school? It's supposed to be a really pretty campus. I wonder what the dorms look like."

Lexi sat on her bed shaking her head. If she lived to be a million years old, she'd never quite figure out how Egg and Binky worked. But how-ever unusual their relationship, it did work. Bin-ky's face was glowing at the thought of visiting her brother, and no doubt Egg would be happy about it, as well.

But at the moment it was too early to think about the mind-bending McNaughtons. As Binky chattered, Lexi fell back onto her pillows and cov-ered her head with her blanket.

When the doorbell rang, Lexi groaned and rolled out of bed. She pulled on her bathrobe and was searching for her slippers when their guest came bounding up the stairs.

Egg skidded to a halt in the doorway. He was beaming like a lighthouse and carrying a dozen long-stemmed red roses in his arm.

"Wow!" Binky's eyes grew wide. "They're beautiful! I've never had that many roses in my whole life," she added wistfully.

"Angela's a lucky girl," Lexi said, referring to Egg's girlfriend. "They're for her, aren't they?"

"Maybe. Maybe not," Egg said slyly as he gently set down the roses. "But never mind that, I've got great news."

Lexi glanced at Binky, wondering if that would throw her into another depression, but Binky seemed only curious.

"What?"

"I got another scholarship for school—enough to pay my room and board for the year! I think Mom and Dad are still dancing around the kitchen table over this one. And I can use my work-study paychecks to save for the following year." Egg's expression softened. "And that means the money they were saving for me can now be applied to *your* college savings account, Binky. Isn't that great?"

"It's like a gift falling out of the sky," Binky murmured. "I haven't said anything, but I've been so worried about there being two of us in college at the same time." She lowered her head. "I thought I might have to go to the junior college and stay at home."

"Oh, Bink," Egg soothed. "You should have said something."

"You mean instead of being a jerk to you?" Binky looked miserable.

"Oh, I'm used to that," Egg said lightly. "I can

read you like a book, sis."

"Hah!" Binky challenged. "What am I thinking right now?"

Egg closed his eyes and screwed his face into an expression of deep thought. When he opened them he said, "You're jealous because you think I bought these flowers for Angela. You like her and it's okay that she get them, but you wish I hadn't come over here to rub it in your face."

Binky's jaw dropped, and Lexi realized immediately that Egg had guessed exactly what Binky was thinking.

"How did you do that?" Binky demanded.

"Give me a little credit. I'm not as dumb as I look, you know."

Fortunately Binky did not have time to retort to that opening. Egg leaned over with a fluorish, picked up the roses, and handed them to his sister. "These are for you. It's my way of saying thank you for being a great sister. Even at your worst, you're pretty special. I'm going to miss you next fall, and I hope you'll hurry up and join me in college."

Tears welled up in Binky's eyes, and Lexi could feel a few in her own. How beautiful. And how unexpected.

Binky flung herself at her tall, skinny brother, knocking him against a wall. She grabbed him at the waist and hugged so tightly that Lexi wondered if Egg would stop breathing.

Then she let go of him, once again nearly making him fall, her attention now on the roses.

"Thank you, Egg. I'm going to keep them forever. I'll press them in books, and when my kids get big enough to read, they'll find the petals in the pages, and I can tell them how very sweet their uncle Egg really is."

"You'd do that?" Egg was surprised and pleased.

"Of course. Come home with me now and help me arrange them in water. I'm going to call everyone I know and have them come look at my flowers."

Binky left the room holding the roses like a queen, with Egg, her loyal subject, trailing behind.

When Lexi heard the door slam downstairs and she knew they were gone, she burst into a fit of laughter. Then she glanced at the clock. Now it really was time to get up. Today was the day she'd promised to visit her grandmother.

Chapter Nine

Todd found Lexi in the family room at the nursing home where her grandmother lived. The shades were drawn and the lights out. She was sitting in the overstuffed chair she always used when visiting her grandmother.

"I wondered if I'd find you here," Todd said softly. "I've looked everywhere else."

"Why?" The word was curious but detached, as if it came from someone other than Lexi, someone who was genuinely curious why Todd had made the effort.

He pulled up a stool and sat down in front of her. "Because we need to talk."

"Do we?" Again the detached air.

"Lexi, don't do this. I really need to talk to you." His voice was pleading.

"I haven't seen you since graduation night. I don't know why you should be in such a hurry to see me now." There was no accusation in her voice, only pain.

"I need to explain—"

"It doesn't matter. We aren't supposed to be dating anymore. Why should I have to know every detail of your life?"

"I'd like to think you cared."

Lexi finally moved, her eyes blazing. "I don't dare! It hurts too much."

"If you're taking about Megan . . ."

Lexi lowered her eyelids.

". . . and what we did after you left the party . . ."

"Maybe I don't want to hear this." Lexi's voice quivered.

"We had a long talk."

Lexi was tempted to put her hands over her ears, but she didn't move.

"She knows all about you, of course. Just like I know about Loren."

Loren? It was a name Lexi hadn't heard before. She didn't know anyone at Cedar River High with that name.

"Her boyfriend. Ex-boyfriend, actually. He goes to the same school as Megan. Her parents are very strict and thought they were getting too 'close.' Sound familiar?"

Where was he going with this? Lexi wondered. It certainly wasn't the conversation she'd expected to have with him.

"I know it must have felt like I left you and fell for Megan all in a week, but it wasn't that way at all." Todd took a deep breath. "We were drawn to each other, sure, but it was because we were both going through the same situation. And it seemed wiser to hang out with Megan than go against your parents' wishes. Besides, you and Jerry looked awfully comfortable together."

Lexi stared at him. Was Todd trying to say he'd been jealous?

"I've known Jerry forever, Todd. Why shouldn't we be comfortable together? Jerry's like a brother to me. He's grown up. I do like him, but it's the way I like Egg or Tim. Not romantically."

Todd stared at his feet, his shoulders drooped with what appeared to be relief. "I thought maybe . . ."

"So did I . . . about you and Megan, I mean."

"No way!" Todd blurted, then blushed. "And it's not because I didn't try to think of her the way I think of you. It just wouldn't happen."

"I understand. Jerry's become a very sweet guy, but . . ."

"No fireworks?" Todd said with his first hint of humor.

"Not even a sparkler." Lexi could have wept with joy, but then another thought swept through her mind. "So now what are we going to do?"

Todd squared his shoulders. "There's only one thing we can do. Talk to your parents."

"I don't know. . . . They've been pretty happy that we're seeing other people."

"What choice do we have?"

Lexi considered the question. "None. Let's go."

———

Dr. and Mrs. Leighton were sitting in the living room on the big couch holding hands when Todd and Lexi entered. Her mother blushed slightly but didn't move away from her husband. Lexi and Todd exchanged a glance.

"We'd like to talk," Lexi began. "If it's a good time."

"It's always a good time for you, honey. Sit down, both of you." Dr. Leighton didn't appear upset that Todd and Lexi were together; far from it, he seemed almost pleased.

"Dad, Mom, Todd wanted to come here today because we're both miserable. . . ." Lexi began to choke on her tears, and Todd picked up the conversation.

"We've done what you said, stayed apart, dated others. I know it hasn't been very long, but when you're as unhappy as we've been, it seems like forever. We have learned, both of us, some of the things I think you wanted us to learn. There *are* other great people out there. We *can* make new friends. We don't have to date each other exclusively, but that's what we want.

"And," Todd continued with a fond look at Lexi, "we learned some other things, too. Lexi and I are best friends. We miss each other. We have more fun together than we do apart."

"Todd's trying to say we want to spend more time together," Lexi blurted. "It doesn't matter if it's in a big group or alone as a couple. We both like to be with our friends. I know that this summer I want to spend all the time I can with Binky, Jennifer, Anna Marie, Matt, Jerry, and Tim. Next summer we'll be going different ways. But I want Todd to be with us, too. It's wrecked things for everyone, not just us!"

Dr. and Mrs. Leighton looked at each other thoughtfully. Todd hurried to speak, as if afraid he wouldn't have another chance if he didn't talk now.

"We'd like permission to spend more time together. I know you are uncomfortable with that, but Lexi and I did a lot of talking on the way over here. We won't disappoint you. We promise."

"We decided something else," Lexi added. "We'll leave this relationship in God's hands. We can all pray about it, can't we? Wouldn't He be the best one to decide?"

Much to Todd and Lexi's surprise, Dr. Leighton burst out laughing. "You two really are bringing out the big guns, aren't you?"

Lexi blushed. "I guess I was being a little dramatic."

"But it means a lot to us to be together with our friends—and with each other. Of course, if you say no . . ." Todd looked grim.

Dr. Leighton stretched and put his big, gentle hands behind his head. "It is pretty hard to say no to such a compelling argument."

"It is?" Lexi and Todd chimed, amazed.

"Besides, your mom and I have been impressed with how hard you've both tried to obey us—and how hard it's been on both of you to do so. You've proven a lot to us. You are responsible, sensible teenagers. Kids we can trust.

"Understand that it doesn't mean we've completely changed our minds. We wanted you to realize how very young you are and what a big world is out there for you to discover. But we also don't want to ruin precious friendships."

"So we can spend more time together?" Lexi asked hopefully.

"Well, I wouldn't want to be the one who ultimately broke up the gang," Lexi's father admitted. "We've become awfully fond of these kids."

Dr. Leighton made a strangled noise as Lexi flung her arms around his neck and squeezed. "Oh, Daddy, you do understand!"

As her father pried her arms off his neck, he chuckled. "Even though when I was your age dinosaurs roamed the earth?"

"You aren't that old!" Lexi paused for effect. "Are you?"

Todd and Lexi left the Leightons' feeling a whole lot better than they had when they arrived.

"Let's go to the McNaughtons'. They'll be glad to hear the news," Lexi suggested.

"Egg will make us help him pack," Todd warned. "Jennifer and Matt were trapped there earlier."

"Then let's call everyone to help. We've been together this long, there's no use stopping now."

Then Lexi turned pensive. "I've been very blessed here in Cedar River. I guess God did know what He was doing when He allowed us to move here."

"He usually does know best, doesn't He?"

Todd and Lexi joined hands and walked together toward the McNaughtons'.

Epilogue

Had it already been a year since Egg's graduation? *Must be*, Lexi mused, since today was hers. She stood in the hallway outside the gymnasium surrounded by restless classmates waiting for more instructions before entering the wide doors of the gym to the strain of "Pomp and Circumstance" for the most exciting walk of their lives so far.

Binky, her small face glowing, dashed up to Lexi in her oversized gown. "I just peeked out front. Egg made it! He and my parents just arrived from the airport. Lexi, he's gotten taller."

"Oh my." Lexi imagined a skyscraper with Egg's bony frame.

"And fat!"

"What?" Lexi stared at her friend. "Egg?"

"Well, maybe not fat, but heavier. He looks good. Older too. Imagine that. I thought my brother would never grow up!"

"Who's growing up?" Todd entered the conversation looking more handsome than usual in his cap and gown. "Not me."

"You've always been a grown-up, Todd," Binky pointed out. "Mature. Stable. Sensible. None of the things that described Egg."

"But doesn't he look great now?" Angela joined the group. Her eyes were dreamy. Though they'd agreed to date others, Angela and Egg had kept in touch by email, and she'd been looking forward to his homecoming ever since his last visit at Christmas.

"What's this? A family reunion?" Matt, Tim, and Jerry sauntered up beside them. Matt wore his mortarboard far back on his head and at a slightly rebellious tilt. He was looking happier than usual because his entire family was present for graduation and getting along well—all for his sake.

Even Jerry's parents were there with the aunt and uncle who'd virtually raised him while his parents were working out of the country. Happiness glowed on his features.

"I did it! I made it!" Jennifer came racing up to them, cap in hand, blond hair flying. "I'm actually going to graduate!"

"We never doubted it for a minute," Lexi said.

"But I did. I was sure my dyslexia would keep me at Cedar River High until I was so old they would just put me in a trophy case somewhere for visitors to gawk at. I can still see it, 'Oldest Living Non-Graduate.' "

"Guess you'll have to put your dream for that on hold, Jen. There's a diploma in that stack for you somewhere."

"Where's Anna Marie?" Tim wondered.

"Right here, behind you." Anna Marie tugged on her gown. "Why is my gown so short and yours so long, Binky? You look like a hot air balloon with a head, and I look like I went swimming in this thing and shrunk it!"

"Do we have time to trade gowns?"

"If we hurry."

The pair rushed off together.

"Just think," Binky sighed. "Our last day together."

"I doubt that," Todd retorted. "Don't we have plans to go tubing this summer?"

"And camping?"

"And horseback riding?"

"And a big party before we all go to college?"

"Well, yes, but . . ."

"Don't get mushy on us now," Lexi ordered. "I don't want my mascara to run before we walk down the aisle."

Suddenly a shriek of happiness split the air and Peggy appeared through a cluster of students. She was grinning from ear to ear.

"You made it!" Lexi flung her arms around her friend. "I'm so glad!"

"I wouldn't have missed it for anything." She stood back. "You guys look so good!"

The band began to tune up in the gym.

"And I'm coming to every one of your house parties," Peggy assured them. "But I have to know now—what's everyone doing in the fall?"

"Cedar River Junior College," Tim said. "Anna Marie is going there, too."

"Binky and I are both going to the same school Egg attends," Angela said. "We both got scholarships and work study. We're going to be roommates."

"Super!" Peggy enthused. "What about the Hi-Fives?"

"Minda is going to the university with a couple of the others. They are already talking about taking the sororities by storm. Gina is going to beauty school."

"I'm going to work for a year," Matt said. "Then, when I've saved some money, I'm going to Bible school. If I like it, I might go into the ministry. I'd like to work with gangs and troubled kids."

"Awesome!"

Lexi named the private Christian all-women's school she'd been accepted to.

"And I'm going to be right across the river in the men's school," Todd added.

"That means they live and study apart but get to have parties together," Jennifer explained.

"And what about you?" Peggy turned to Jennifer.

"I don't know yet," Jennifer admitted. "School isn't my best thing because I read and write so slowly. But I do like kids, so I'm going to work at a day care this summer, and if it doesn't drive me crazy, I might go into early childhood development. Now, what are you doing?"

Peggy grinned. "I've been accepted at Harvard! Can you believe it? Apparently someone there thinks I'm a math whiz. I'm not going to argue. It's going to be tough, but anything worth having is worth working for, don't you think?"

As her friends chatted about their plans, Lexi closed her eyes and gave a silent prayer of thanks. She had been blessed. Good friends. A good school. A family who loved her.

Then the first strains of the march sifted down the hallway. Binky and Anna Marie bolted out of the ladies' room in swapped gowns and hurried into line and the group began to take their walk. Lexi didn't know where her life's road would lead, but she did know that God would always be with her.

A Note From Judy

I'm glad you're reading *Cedar River Daydreams*! I hope I've given you something to think about as well as a story to entertain you. If you feel you have any of the problems that Lexi and her friends experience, I encourage you to talk with your parents, a pastor, or a trusted adult friend. There are many people who care about you!

I love to hear from my readers, so if you'd like to receive my newsletter and a bookmark, please send a self-addressed, stamped envelope to:

Judy Baer
Bethany House Publishers
11400 Hampshire Avenue South
Minneapolis, MN 55438

Be sure to look for my *Dear Judy . . .* books at your local bookstore. These books are full of questions that you, my readers, have asked in your letters, along with my response. Just about every topic is covered—from dating and romance to friendships and parents. Hope to hear from you soon!

Dear Judy, What's It Like at Your House?
Dear Judy, Did You Ever Like a Boy
    (who didn't like you?)

Live! From Brentwood High

1 • Risky Assignment
2 • Price of Silence
3 • Double Danger
4 • Sarah's Dilemma
5 • Undercover Artists
6 • Faded Dreams

Other Books by Judy Baer

- Dear Judy, What's It Like at Your House?
- Dear Judy, Did You Ever Like a Boy (who didn't like you?)
- Paige
- Pamela

Young Adult Fiction Series From Bethany House Publishers
(Ages 12 and up)

———⚬⚬⚬———

CEDAR RIVER DAYDREAMS • by Judy Baer
Experience the challenges and excitement of high school life with Lexi Leighton and her friends.

GOLDEN FILLY SERIES • by Lauraine Snelling
Tricia Evanston races to become the first female jockey to win the sought-after Triple Crown.

JENNIE MCGRADY MYSTERIES • by Patricia Rushford
A contemporary Nancy Drew, Jennie McGrady's sleuthing talents bring back readers again and again.

LIVE! FROM BRENTWOOD HIGH • by Judy Baer
The staff of an action-packed teen-run news show explores the love, laughter, and tears of high school life.

PASSPORT TO DANGER • by Mary Reeves Bell
Constantine Rea, an American living in modern-day Austria, confronts the lasting horrors of the Holocaust.

THE SPECTRUM CHRONICLES • by Thomas Locke
Adventure awaits readers in this fantasy series set in another place and time.

SPRINGSONG BOOKS • by various authors
Compelling love stories and contemporary themes promise to capture the hearts of readers.

UNMISTAKABLY COOPER ELLIS • by Wendy Lee Nentwig
Laugh and cry with Cooper as she strives to balance modeling, faith, and life at her Manhattan high school.

WHITE DOVE ROMANCES • by Yvonne Lehman
Romance, suspense, and fast-paced action for teens committed to finding pure love.